BITE OF LOYALTY

BLOOD OATH

BOOK ONE

R.L. CAULDER

WHITE RABBIT PUBLISHING

Cover by: Luminescence Covers

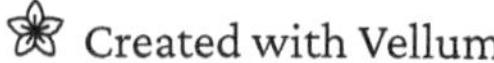

DEDICATION

To the women who are tired of running from their demons in fear, so they turn to look them in the face and smile instead.

"Roses are red, violets are blue, here comes Alina, and she's going to kill you." *-Alina Van Helsing, Bite of Loyalty.*

P.S.- Thank you to the Peen Queens for letting me use their names for some characters in this book. I adore you all.

I

ALINA

Letting my hips gyrate to the pulsing bass of the music, my head tipped back as I closed my eyes and soaked in the moment. My body was buzzing with the steady flow of alcohol, making it easy to numb the unwelcome thoughts swirling in my head. I felt as close to the freedom I so desperately wanted as I'd probably ever get right now.

At this moment, I wasn't the sole Van Helsing heir.

I wasn't expected to take over the head of house position to govern all slayers.

I wasn't expected to find a suitable slayer to marry to continue our family legacy.

I was just a twenty-one-year-old girl, celebrating her birthday with friends. I would probably regret taking all those shots tomorrow morning, but that was for future Alina to worry about.

Right now I would focus on enjoying this time with my girls.

There weren't many places in Sanguis to celebrate my birthday at, with slayers owning only a small section of the vampire territory, but when you were a few drinks deep, anywhere could be a party with the right people at your side.

It was easy to sway the bartender to hook up my phone to their speakers so that my favorite playlist boomed through the empty establishment. I was more than thankful that all the slayers our age who were typically out this late were seemingly at home resting, saving their livers for the "real" birthday party my parents were hosting at our estate tomorrow.

It was a little odd, seeing as slayers were typically the epitome of the human saying "YOLO"—you only live once. They lived each day like it was their last because it very well could be in our line of work. It came with the territory of being the supernatural police of the blood-suckers who couldn't seem to keep their fangs to themselves and procreated like bunnies in heat.

But I supposed when they were all expected to be in the Van Helsing estate and in front of the leaders of our society, being presented to their daughter, they cared a little bit more about being in tip-top shape. Wouldn't want to turn up to the "real" party looking disheveled because you partied too late the night before.

Blearily glancing at the clock on the wall, I rolled my eyes. Scratch that—the real party was today, seeing as it was near two a.m. now.

Another hour closer to being tied to a fate I didn't want. *Yippie.*

An arm slid around my waist, and one of my best friend's signature cherry blossom perfume wrapped around me. "I love you, Skye," I mumbled as I enclosed her slight frame in a hug, making her sway to the music in time with me. She let me guide her as she giggled with her face in my chest.

She was fun-sized, and if I could fit her in my pocket and carry around her sunny disposition with me at all times, I totally would. She balanced my more bleak and reserved outlook on life.

"I love tipsy you, babe," she yelled up at me, face squashed in my tits. "You're so sweet when you're like this, and you know I love your face times a million."

Dropping my cheek to rest on the top of her head, I murmured, "I love you too," as I squeezed her a little tighter.

I wasn't one to be openly affectionate, either physically or with my words, so she was really getting the best version of me.

"I can't wait for the three of us to be spinster slayers who disappoint our parents for refusing a match."

Her words were a minor buzzkill, but I tried to hold back the groan at the reminder of all of our fates. *If only being a spinster were a viable option.* I would take it in a heartbeat and even adopt a bunch of cats to complete the lifestyle.

It felt like such an archaic tradition for slayers to be married by twenty-one to ensure our kind lived on. Our population, while not large in comparison to the vampires' ever-expanding one, was a highly skilled and trained group that was nowhere close to extinction.

And the thought that marriage equaled babies was ridiculous for multiple reasons. One being that not everyone wanted children and shouldn't be pressured to have them, and two, people can fuck and have kids without marriage.

Complete shocker, I know.

While we were all gifted with the blood running through our veins, the minor drawback was that it was harder to get pregnant for slayer women than typical humans. So the logic of the elders who established our laws was that if they ensured a union at a young age, it would encourage the couple to start trying at a younger age, giving them many fertile years together.

It honestly disgusted me if I thought about it long enough. I was never one of those women who saw myself as a mother. Hell, I couldn't even picture myself as a girlfriend to anyone right now. When I thought of the future, I imagined myself running point on missions and assisting my parents in leading the slayers. And in my down time, I'd be the really cool aunt to my best friends' kids if they wanted them. That was enough for me.

Despite my best efforts, a frustrated groan bubbled out of me as I lifted my cheek off of her head. "Don't remind me."

I hoped I could bring some change to the archaic slayer traditions once I was head of our house. It was the only positive part of taking on the role, in my opinion. I didn't care about the reverence or the power, but if it was going to be forced on me, I was going to use it for change.

The only part of the forced matching ceremony that I was thankful for was that we didn't follow the human tradition of the woman being taken in by the man's family and taking his last name. The slayer who was the most powerful would take their new partner into their House, no matter their gender.

I would, at the very least, be able to stay in my home and remain Alina Van Helsing. Nothing could take that from me. It was who I would remain until the day death came to hold me in its gnarled, cold grasp.

"I'm sorry, Alina. You know if I could change this for you, I would in a heartbeat," she answered. Her somber tone matched how my heart felt at its core, despite being in the best company a girl could ask for.

It felt like the end of my freedom was drawing nearer with what the party entailed. Eligible men from each of the Houses would present their hand in marriage to me. If any of them had a fucking spine and didn't bow to my every whim or desire because of who I was, perhaps that would be a welcome idea. If I was to be tied to someone for the rest of my life, I wanted a man who would challenge me if I was wrong. Who would help me grow as a person and bring out the best in me. I knew I was a handful, but as my grandmother once told me, "Never dim your shine for someone who thinks they're going to be burned by your greatness. The right person for you will put on sunglasses and bask in your glow."

Skye pulled back from my arms, her big silver eyes swirling with compassion. "You're going to have to choose one of the potential matches tomorrow, Alina. I know we joke about it, but if you don't decide, your parents will."

And therein lay the true problem. Tomorrow wasn't optional, no matter how many tears I shed. My parents tried to reassure me, saying there had to be at least one slayer I would get along with, and that perhaps it would be a whirlwind romance like their match had been.

My father was quite the bachelor and hadn't wanted to be tied down, but from the moment my mom approached him on his match day, he had eyes for only her. If I didn't see the love they held for each other every day, I would've said that shit only happened in fairy tales or romance books. But still, I was under no misguided notion that everyone could have that same dream ending.

"I think I need another shot," I announced, shaking my head to clear away the depressing thoughts, feeling my buzz beginning to wear off.

Jade sashayed toward us from the bar, returning after having announced she was paying our tab a few minutes ago. She threw her arms around both of our shoulders. "I think it's time to get her royal pain in the ass home."

Narrowing my eyes at my other best friend and letting out a menacing growl, I snapped my teeth at her as if I had vampire fangs, drawing laughs from both of them. Then I sighed heavily, letting some of my resentment bleed into my tone. "But that means I'm closer to going to sleep and waking up to the worst day of my life."

"Okay, Chomper," Jade relented, her bright blue eyes full of sadness. "A couple more songs but no more drinks. Fair?"

They both understood my position, seeing as their own matches were only a few months away. It had been us against the world for so long, and sure we'd had some passing flings here and there, but no one had held our attention for long.

"Fine," I huffed, disentangling myself from the girls who'd been by my side since we were first introduced at school.

Thankfully, slayers started training from a young age. As the only child in the Van Helsing home, I probably would've remained isolated and alone for far too much of my life otherwise. My parents were the youngest couple in our family, and I was doted on subsequently. While I loved my family, I still needed time away with friends.

There were numerous slayer family lines, but the Van Helsing House was the original and therefore ruling House. With that came a wide berth from the other Houses, supposedly out of respect, but it always felt more like a mixture of fear and resentment to me.

Skye and Jade were the only kids who hadn't kept their distance or whispered about me behind my back on that first day, and we'd been inseparable ever since. I called them my best friends, but at this point, they were more like sisters.

Crossing over to the speakers, I grabbed my phone with the intention of finding one of my favorite songs, to end this night with a bang. But as the screen lit up, dozens of missed calls and text messages greeted me. Jade, Skye, and I had agreed to put our phones on "Do Not Disturb" so that our last hoorah before my doomsday would be uninterrupted.

Alarm bells went off in my head, and I called out sharply, "Guys! Check your phones!"

My mind was foggy from alcohol, struggling to

understand the extent of what was happening, but two words stuck out that made all the blood in my body turn ice cold: *vampire attack*.

That sobered me up quickly, a rush of adrenaline replacing any remaining intoxication. Ripping the aux cord out of my phone, I ran toward the exit, heart pounding loudly in my ears. Skye and Jade called my name behind me, begging me to wait, to formulate a plan and meet up with other slayers, but I didn't stop. I couldn't. I had to get home. I had to do something.

How had the vampires broken through our wards? The witches from Carmina had put them up, and my parents paid an exorbitant amount of money each year to have them strengthened and maintained. It should've been tighter than a virgin asshole to get through. Like the veils between the planes of existence, it was set to only allow certain beings through it–with this one tied to slayer DNA.

Tears blurred my vision as I tried to call every family member in my home, screaming into the eerie silence of the night when no one picked up.

"Answer me!" I yelled, sobs choking me as the last ring sounded and my mom's voicemail picked up again. Throwing my useless fucking phone to the ground, I sliced my nail into the palm of my hand, letting a tiny drop of blood spill as I called my soul sword to me. "*Devorare.*"

As slayers, our soul weapons were the only magic we were able to tap into. The weapons weren't something we chose—they chose us. We received them in a coming-of-age ceremony where we spilled our blood and recited the ancient slayer code, swearing our fealty to the cause. The magic didn't find everyone worthy of wielding a soul weapon, though those not chosen remained slayers nonetheless.

Those blessed with a weapon were revered for their skill in battle, with their history recorded for all future holders of their soul weapons to read and learn from. Each weapon could be wielded by only one slayer at a time, but when their life came to an end, it disappeared until it found the next worthy master.

My eyes flicked down to the flaming red sword. It burned brightly in the dark of night, and I worried about my lack of understanding of her. There was no recorded history of a sword with the name *Devour*, so I was flying blind trying to understand what exactly I wielded. I'd only had her for a week, and to say it wasn't going well was an understatement.

I called to the piece of us that was tethered intrinsically, hoping she would hear my plea.

Please, lend me your strength, Devorare. I need you now more than ever.

The wrought iron fence surrounding my home came into view, and the sight of decapitated bodies displayed on it, spikes protruding from their chests and bellies, nearly brought me to my knees. A strangled cry tore from my throat as I passed through the open gate and toward the marble stairs leading into my home. Wrapping my hand around my hilt tightly, my mind cleared a fraction as I let myself fall into the slayer mindset that had been drilled into me since birth.

Calm yourself. Tumultuous emotions can lead to your death and the deaths of those around you.

Focus. You cannot afford to become distracted for even one second, lest you give your enemy the opening they need.

Trust in your comrades to handle their part of the mission.

I slowed as I passed through the once-white front doors, now splattered with blood, scanning the foyer and keeping my breathing light in an effort to calm my racing heart. If any vampires remained, the organ beating loudly in my chest would practically offer them a meal on a silver platter.

The creak of a door sounded on the second floor, and the hairs on the back of my neck stood on end as a chill crept through my body. Slowly ascending the steps, my body tensed in preparation of an attack, but none came as I reached the top. I swiveled my head around, scanning for any indication of where the sound came from.

"A—Alina..." my mother's voice called, shattering my focus. I rushed toward the end of the hall, in the direction where the strangled word came from.

"Mom!" I cried as I dropped my sword to the ground, shoving away the splintered door that covered her body. Falling to my knees, I clutched her hand as I bit my bottom lip harshly. My eyes burned as tears fell, unable to hold them at bay as I took in the blood pouring from the gaping wound in her neck. A large chunk had been torn away by fangs, a death sentence for any slayer. We had some enhanced physical ability, with strength and sight topping that list, but we didn't possess rapid healing capabilities.

My lips trembled as reality sunk in. My mother

was seconds away from death, and there was nothing I could do about it.

I couldn't wrap my brain around how this had happened. Never in the centuries that slayers had occupied Sanguis had an attack like this been successful. How had they been caught off guard? How many vampires had been here? How had we not seen any as they passed through the streets near where we were drinking to reach the houses?

While I had been drinking and feeling sorry for myself, they had been fighting for their lives.

Her inhale of breath was strangled and wet, squelching with the liquid filling her lungs. A deep rattling rose from her chest as she focused on the ceiling and rasped out, "Infected."

My breathing stopped. Infected with poison or with vampire venom?

I was already shaking my head, trying to deny the second possibility, before she confirmed it with her next words. "Kill me."

Part of our vow as slayers was that we would never allow one of our kind to be turned. It was a fate worse than death.

"I can't, Mom," I choked out. My body shook, and tears dropped onto her face as I leaned over her body, cradling her to my chest. I couldn't picture a world without her in it.

"You..." she breathed out, her lips next to my ear, "must."

My sobs of agony were no longer something I could contain as they ripped out of me, echoing through our home.

Her body convulsed in my arms. This was the last chance I had before her heart stopped and the venom changed her. I couldn't fail her in her last moments–I couldn't live with that guilt for the rest of my life. Slayers believed if we were changed through vampire venom, our souls would no longer be welcomed into our ancestral resting place.

With a scream of heartbreak, I laid her down and picked up my sword. I stood, placing the tip of my blade between her ribs and lining it up perfectly with her heart. "I love you, Mom," I said between choked sobs. "I'm sorry."

Sliding the sword into her chest, I saw the relief fill her eyes before they dulled, life leeching out of them completely.

My mother was dead.

I had driven my sword into her heart.

It was like switching into a cold trance and operating on autopilot. I checked out mentally, incapable of handling the emotions crashing through me after losing her and all of those I'd seen slain outside.

Pulling my sword from her chest, I realized that if she had been infected, it was likely that more of my family had been as well. I stood no chance against them if they turned and I had to fight them alone.

I had to search our home for any survivors or victims, though. As the new head of the Van Helsing House, this was my duty. If any of them were on the edge, as my mother had been, I had to grant their souls peace in death.

As I looked over my shoulder to begin my search, my mouth opened to scream as three hooded figures stood before me. The closest figure gripped my face harshly enough to make me wince, my teeth drawing blood as they pressed into the insides of my cheeks. The other two figures grabbed my wrists, snapping them and making me cry out in pain as I dropped my sword.

"Dracula sends his regards," a raspy voice announced before yanking my head to the side and sinking his fangs into my neck.

Searing, white-hot pain blossomed through me for a few agonizing moments until the world went dark.

2

ALINA

My mind blanked, drifting aimlessly through an endlessly dark void until I plummeted, free falling through space and slamming back into consciousness with a jerk. Nausea rolled through me as my extremities came to life, pulsating with soreness.

My vision blurred as I opened my eyes, and I hissed in pain at the ferocity of the light that blinded me. Pain rolled through my head in relentless waves, disorientating me as I grappled for the ground beneath me.

"Fuck," I groaned, focusing on the rough texture of the floor as I pushed myself up, keeping my eyes closed.

"Alina!" a voice called. The sound echoed through my head painfully, clanging around like a fucking gong in a large, empty room.

I grumbled as I swayed.

The voice was familiar, yet I couldn't think of who it belonged to. I tried to open my eyes once more, slitting my left eye slightly and regretting it in an instant. It felt like the world was spinning on a new axis that I couldn't orient myself with. Bile churned in my stomach, threatening to come up. Arms hooked under my armpits, pulling me to my feet before wrapping around my waist. I placed my arm around their shoulder, helping bear the brunt of my weight as I wobbled with the new position.

Then a smell assaulted my nose, and a moan bubbled out of my throat as my senses roared back to life. It was unlike anything I'd ever experienced. My mind suddenly turned razor sharp, focusing solely on pinpointing the source of the smell.

I needed it. It would make me feel better, I knew it.

Letting my nose guide me, I nuzzled into the place the scent was the strongest, and a rhythmic, pulsating beat accompanied it. The voice that said what I thought was my name once more.

That was my name, right? Alina. It rang true in my

head, but I couldn't find it in me to give a fuck to see what the person wanted. They could wait until I felt better.

Shaking my head to clear the voice, I sank back into the hunt for the scent. My tongue darted out as my mouth opened to welcome the source of promised bliss. It was like finding the gates of heaven, tasting whatever this was. I swore angels sang in my head as light shone upon me. Strength filled me as I surged for more.

Thick warmth coated my mouth like honey as I held tightly to the source that was thrashing around in my grasp, trying to escape. I couldn't let it leave. I felt better with each drop consumed. A menacing growl ripped from me as I doubled down, sucking hard to get as much as I could before my prey escaped. Thankfully it stilled quickly, and euphoria coursed through me as I drank my fill.

The feeling of my strength returning in full, coursing through me, but my breath caught in my throat when I realized I felt stronger than ever before. It was a heady feeling that I couldn't get enough of. I felt so powerful, like I could take on an army of vampires alone.

Wait, this wasn't right.

Vampires.

Slayers.

I was a slayer.

Alina Van Helsing.

A chill ran through my body. I faltered, the dome of bliss surrounding my mind popping like a bubble. The voice from before rasped, "Alina, no."

Skye. That was Skye's voice that had been calling to me.

Opening my eyes and blinking rapidly to clear the fog, I screamed at what lay before me. Blood coated my best friend, who lay cradled in my arms, limp. Twin puncture wounds in her throat gushed blood, and I rushed to staunch the flow with my hand until I could find something better.

Her big grey eyes stared up at me in fear, and it felt like a rock sinking in my stomach as memories crashed into me with a vengeance. *I had found my family home in shambles, and my mother was infected. I had killed her...and then...and then three vampires had overtaken me and sank their fangs into me.*

"Dracula sends his regards."

"Skye," I whispered. My voice wobbled, thick with emotion, as the understanding of what I had done crashed into me. Fangs pressed into my lower lip. *What I'd become.*

A tear fell from the corner of her eye as she

whimpered, wriggling to escape my grip, but she was barely able to lift her arm even a fraction. My heart shattered, splinters of the fragmented, broken organ flying uselessly around me as pain lanced through me.

Tears burned my eyes, and I tilted my head back, screaming out my rage as they flowed over my cheeks. My body shook as I sobbed, crying out for anyone to help.

"Help us," I cried. "Please!"

But who could fix what had happened?

I was a fucking bloodsucker that had sealed my best friend's fate.

"Alina! Oh my god, what happened?"

Jade's voice echoed through the foyer, dragging my attention away from Skye as she came skidding through the blood-stained front doors of my crumbled home. My head fell forward as I stared down at Skye, choking on a sob as I realized there was no spark of life in her eyes.

She was gone.

Agony coursed through me at the loss that had likely devastated our town tonight, and the hand I now played in it. I didn't even know the full implication of this breach of security, unsure if the attack extended to other Houses, but I assumed if my own was hit this hard, it wasn't going to be good.

How many slayers were left?

Was I the only one to be turned?

Cradling Skye's limp body to my chest, I breathed in her cherry blossom scent for what would be the last time and hot tears rolled down my face, dripping into her hair. Emotion clogged my throat as I whispered, "I'm so sorry, Skye. I'm so fucking sorry."

I could feel then that the fracture within my soul would never be repaired.

Jade gasped as she sank to her knees next to me. Her voice wobbled as she ran her hand along my back in what should have been a soothing gesture, but truly felt like scalding iron running over my flesh. "I can't believe this," she cried.

The sympathy and silent support she lent were things I didn't deserve, and I couldn't fucking stand it for another second.

After gently placing Skye back on the ground, I lunged to my feet, shocked at the speed with which I managed to turn and glare at Jade. "Don't pity me. I did this, Jade."

Her skin paled, mouth widening in horror as she stared up at me. A mirror wasn't necessary to know she was seeing red eyes and a bloody mouth. She raised her hands to cover her mouth, tears slipping down her face, and I shook my head as coldness washed through me.

There was no solace for me in the fact that I hadn't deployed my venom into Skye somehow. It should've given me some peace of mind that she hadn't been turned, especially when I was out of my mind with bloodlust.

I felt nothing but disgust and hatred for myself.

Jade's eyes swirled with confusion, the reality of the moment not quite sinking in for her, and my heart thudded with the knowledge that I needed to actually explain what had taken place here.

Even to my own ears, my voice sounded detached and icy as I gave her a quick, dirty summary. "I was caught off guard after having to kill my own mother before she could turn. Three vampires trapped and bit me before saying, 'Dracula sends his regards.' I woke up in a haze, not knowing fully who I was or where I was. I attacked Skye and drained her."

I saw the moment she stopped considering me her friend, her agony turning to burning rage as she pushed to her feet.

I was no longer her sister in heart. I was the

enemy. Just like that, in the same span of time it would take to turn on a light switch.

I'd lost everyone that mattered to me in one fell swoop, and suddenly my previous anger at having to be matched to another slayer seemed so damn insignificant. What I wouldn't give for an arranged marriage to be my main concern now. To have my family and friends safe. To not have my soul damned and stained with the blood of people I loved.

I didn't deserve to live after what I'd done. After what I'd become.

"Kill me, Jade," I said, holding my hands wide in a welcoming gesture. Closing my eyes, I felt peace with the knowledge that this was the end.

I wouldn't be joining my ancestors in the after-life, but a swift death was better than being alive and a monster.

I couldn't live with the pain that was slowly seeping through the numb front I was desperately clinging to.

I couldn't stand to hear my mother's strangled breaths as she begged me to kill her, the memory on repeat for the rest of this miserable existence.

I couldn't bear to see Skye's wide grey eyes as she stared at me in horror in the nightmares I knew would haunt me every time I closed my eyes.

I couldn't endure the memory of the feeling of the last shred of my heart going up in flames as the last person alive that I loved looked at me in disgust before disowning me.

There was too much guilt to suffer. Too much grief to weather.

I waited for her blade to sink into my neck, but as the seconds ticked by, I lost the calm energy I'd found with the acceptance of my inevitable death. Snapping my eyes open, I found Jade staring at me, unmoving.

"Kill me!" I roared, taking a menacing step forward in an attempt to provoke her.

I *needed* this. She *had* to do this.

She didn't even flinch. Instead, she shook her head, black curls loosely bouncing against her neck as she spared me a glance full of pity. "No. Leave this city, Alina, and never come back."

Her words sank into my brain, and my heart clenched with the realization that she wouldn't grant me this last reprieve.

No. I couldn't be left alive and exiled from the only home I had. Left to deal with this alone, wallowing in grief and self-pity.

Where would I go? I wouldn't join the vampires– I could never answer to their king, Dracula. The monster who had destroyed my life. Who orchestrated the massacre of my loved ones. Who forced my worst nightmare upon me.

As I fell to my knees, the dam on my emotions loosened and broke, leaving me wracking with full-bodied sobs. I cried out, head hanging to allow my silver hair to drape around me like a shield. “Please, Jade. I can’t do this. I can’t live like this.”

There was no warmth to be found in her voice as she spat, “You forgot our most basic rules as slayers. You let your emotions overwhelm you with your mother’s death, Alina. You left yourself unprotected in the middle of an attack, and now Skye is dead because of you. Her death has stained your soul, and that is something you must suffer through. I won’t put you out of your misery–you don’t deserve that kindness.”

Her words tore into my chest, dragging through me like barbed wire.

She was right. I’d abandoned my guard completely despite knowing there was an active attack occurring.

The blame for the deaths this night firmly laid with two people—Dracula for orchestrating the attack, and me for being too weak to protect myself when it mattered.

If Jade wouldn't kill me, I'd find a way to atone for my sins. I'd cut Dracula's head from his body and hope that his minions ripped my head off right after, giving me the release of death I desired.

Shakily pushing to my feet, I kept my gaze down as I asked, "Did any other Houses suffer casualties?"

I needed to understand the scope of loss that had occurred tonight. Before I left, I needed to know if they could rebuild and carry on. Steadfast silence met my ears.

"Please, Jade. I need to know the slayers can recover from this."

The silence stretched long and uncomfortable between us until she finally sighed. Reluctance tinged her voice as she said, "No other Houses were targeted. Van Helsing was the only one."

Had the vampires been tasked with wiping out only my family and turning me? The questions in my head were piling up, and I planned to get my answers from Dracula himself.

How had they broken through the wards?

Why target my family but no others?

Why change me?

Shouts of alarm sounded outside, forcing my head up with a snap. Other Slayers were coming. Sliding my gaze to Jade, I took a step forward out of habit to give her a hug. Her mirrored step back stopped me in my tracks, faltering over the unfamiliarity of the situation we found ourselves in.

"I'm…I'm so sorry, Jade," I whispered, hoping she felt the truth of my words.

Tears lined her eyes as she shook her head. A choked breath pushed through her lips as the tears seeped from her eyes and over her cheeks. "T-tell that to Skye."

Biting down on my bottom lip until my fang punctured my skin, I nodded in understanding. There was nothing left for me to say, so I reached up and swiped away the trickle of blood from my chin as the realization that there was no life left here for me to live really sank in.

With the blood from my punctured lip I traced the Van Helsing emblem of the V trapped within the H on my palm, swearing my final blood oath.

"I will get revenge for the deaths here today."

Turning on my heel I ran, zipping through the house and refusing to look at the fallen bodies of my family and the guards I had come to befriend. As I ran out the back patio and into the unforgiving world, I made a solemn vow to myself and to those lying lifeless behind me.

I would make Dracula regret this if it was the last thing I ever did.

“Roses are red, violets are blue, here comes Alina, and she’s going to kill you,” I murmured as the wind whipped at my face, taking my tears with it before they even had the chance to fall.

3

ALINA

The list of reasons I had to break down felt insurmountable.

My family was slaughtered. I had been forcibly turned into a vampire and killed one of my best friends in the bloodlust I woke in. My other best friend walked away from me, the sting of loss sharp coupled with the fact that I'd lost the only place I'd ever called home too. But even though the list was long, I wouldn't let myself wallow. Trauma processing and coping healthily through my grief weren't my top skills, so I pushed everything to recesses of my mind, avoiding the pain and focusing on the one task that would bring me relief: hunting a vampire.

The possibility that my feelings would one day come back with a vengeance, consuming me whole, was very real. Logically I knew that. But I also knew that I wouldn't be able to put one foot in front of the other if I actually let the floodgates open right now.

Numbing myself to my emotions was the only way I could survive, and that would have to be enough. Because at least being alive meant I could claim my revenge, and then perhaps my soul would find some peace.

Continuing my sprint to the barrier of our territory, I let it all fall away, leaving my thoughts to linger on Dracula and how I could get to him.

His castle sat on the outer edge of Sanguis' territory, tucked away in the mountains, and I knew better than anyone that it would be impossible to get into it. I'd have to pass through countless cities, crossing paths with each nest that was ruled by loyal subjects to Dracula, and it would only get harder from there.

Not a single slayer in all of our history had managed to complete a successful reconnaissance mission to his castle and return to relay what they'd seen. I'd be flying completely blind, and without the backing of a nest to use as a shield to slip past their defenses undetected, it would be damn near impossible.

Hell, I wasn't even sure if just any level of vampire was welcomed into his castle. There was a very good chance it was on an invite-only basis for those who were permitted within the stronghold.

As the edge of our territory came into view, I slowed. The ward flared brightly, rippling in a semi-translucent kaleidoscope of colors. It seemed perfectly intact. Coming to a halt, my eyes swept across it, searching for a weak point.

If that many vampires had managed to come through, how was it still intact?

It couldn't be...could it? That would create a war, though.

My eyebrows furrowed as I considered the only other way the vampires could have gotten in without the whole ward shattering...A witch had to have helped them–a very powerful one at that–if they were able to create an opening that didn't destroy the ward entirely.

Stepping forward to pass through the ward and continue out of our territory, I let out a hiss of pain as my hand connected with the ward and leaped back. Glancing down, my brows creased as I gazed at my hand. The skin blistered and bled, burned from the barrier I had passed through hundreds of times before.

Of course I couldn't get through anymore...no longer would my blood signify me as a slayer. The stark reminder burned even worse than the wound on my hand.

I paced in front of the barrier like an agitated cat, unsure of how to get out. The pain lessened as a chill spread through my hand, and I stopped to stare at it in wonder as the dead skin flaked away, revealing fresh, smooth skin beneath. Blinking, I tried to process this new ability with an open mind, but I couldn't help but look at the skin in anger.

"Why?" I asked, scoffing as I tipped my head back and glared at the sky. The first rays of light peeked through the horizon, but my scowl only deepened. "Why do I deserve to have anything healed after what I did?"

From behind me, a gentle, coaxing voice asked, "Why wouldn't you deserve it?"

Spinning around, I instinctually sliced my nail into my palm in case I needed to call my blade to me. Not for the first time, I found myself grateful that our blades could be called to us anywhere. There was some magic involved that I definitely didn't understand, but they couldn't be wielded by anyone other than their bonded slayer and disappeared when they weren't needed.

I sized up the woman who had appeared near me, seemingly out of thin air. The space behind her reflected back at me, swirling like water in the air with a silver-blue hue distorting the air. It looked like one of the portals we used to go into the human realm when we were alerted to a vampire sighting on the plane of Ordinarius.

Curled blonde hair accentuated an impeccable outfit. The woman wore a black skirt and silky blouse, paired with black heels that gave her a few inches over me. An air of kindness radiated from her stunningly bright, albeit pale, blue eyes.

I could smell the sweetness of her blood, and a shiver ran through me. I wasn't sure how, but I could feel that there was more power in her blood than with Skye or Jade. It called to me like a siren song, and I clenched my eyes shut as my throat dried out, demanding I claim her blood to fuel myself.

Normally, I might have welcomed her company, sensing no threat from her, but right now, I felt like I could trust no one—not even myself.

Ignoring her question, I rebutted with my own. "Who are you?"

Her lips turned up in a smile as she clasped her hands together in front of her. “My name is Estrid. I’m the headmistress at Dark Imaginarium Academy.”

The name rang a bell in my head. The academy resided in the middle of all of the supernatural territories here on Praeditus. It was a neutral ground of sorts, with all of the species mixing there for training.

“Why are you here?” I bit out, on guard and suspicious after what occurred here. “This isn’t your territory.”

She didn’t miss a beat, her gentle smile an indication that she knew the challenge was coming. Her shoulders shook as she let out a laugh and mumbled, “Man, I’m going to memorize this introduction if the Fates keep bringing me to new students like this.”

Her words made little sense to me. *New student? The Fates?*

Lifting a single brow and tilting my head to the side, I silently urged her to continue.

“I’m a goddess from Divinus, and I have the rare power to pierce the veils between all of our planes of existence. Along with that gift, I was blessed by the three goddesses of fate—Urd, Verdandi, and Skuld

—before taking my position as Headmistress of this academy."

My mouth widened in shock, and I blinked rapidly.

Holy shit, an actual goddess was in front of me. Divinus and the higher beings that existed there weren't a secret nor a mystery to me, but I never thought my path would cross with one.

Estrid's divinity explained the intoxicating scent of her blood, and the knowledge that she was of divine origins helped the fact that power radiated from her aura make more sense to me. My fangs ached as I felt the bloodlust fighting to take over, to fall into the hunt and claim what was mine.

I shook my head, clenching my jaw as I fought off the shadows of the new, darker side of me. It felt like being split into two beings who fought to coexist in one body. Already, I felt like I was failing miserably. How was I supposed to simply exist when I hated this new side of myself? The vampire wasn't who I was at my core. I refused to accept that I could ever coexist with such an ugly part of myself.

Never again will I drink from the vein of another being. Not after what I did to Skye.

If I had to drink blood to survive now, I'd only

consume animal blood. That would work, right? One could only hope.

That vow I made to myself left me feeling stronger, more fortified, and I was able to stave off the primal needs my body demanded. I would fight this, and I would win. Never again would I lose myself to the hunger.

Estrid's eyes traveled the length of my body, and I saw sadness lurking in the depths of her striking eyes. "If there is a student out there who needs my intervention and the fates deem it important, a line is drawn between the person in need and myself. I'm then able to create a portal to draw them into the safety at the academy. It is rare but has occurred twice in as many days. "

She gestured toward the space behind her, proving my assumptions about the portal correct. Her soft, unthreatening tone drew me in, and I found myself wanting to trust her. I didn't want to be in this alone, and I wasn't dumb enough to refuse help if it might get me where I needed to be.

My throat tightened, reminding me that I *would* need to feed soon if I wanted to be the one in control of my hunger in any way. I couldn't be trapped here with the only blood available to me that of my fellow slayers.

My heart panged with the thought. *Could I even consider myself a slayer anymore?*

"Dark Imaginarium Academy is waiting for you," she offered, tone soft and placating in a way that should have eased my distress as I gazed at my home in the distance. "We welcome you into our home."

As my throat tightened, the emotions clawing their way up from my chest threatened to break the fragile control I held over them. I took a deep, steadying breath and glanced back at Estrid, trying to visualize the concept of being a student of Dark Imaginarium Academy.

Accepting Estrid's offer would at least get me out of here, but what could the academy actually offer me? How would it serve my life's mission now? Ending Dracula once and for all is all that mattered. What kind of student would that make me? And what if they kicked me out because I wasn't the type of student they actually wanted? The academy is a means to an end for me, and I highly doubt most students treated this opportunity as such.

"Estrid, I'm not worthy of your protection, or this invite to your academy," I started to explain, gesturing to myself. I was covered in blood, and my eyes, surely reflecting red in the early morning light, made it obvious I was the one responsible for the blood I was covered in.

My voice quivered as I admitted, "I failed my family and friends. I'll likely fail you too. I spent my life devoted to ensuring vampires stayed within the parameters of the law, killing any offenders. What am I supposed to do now that I'm the monster, the offender who needs to be kept away from society?"

Her lips pursed as her eyes bore into mine with a narrow-eyed intensity. I shifted from foot to foot, feeling like she was peering into my soul. No one needed to see the damage inside of me. It was my burden to carry, and I was slowly realizing that I shouldn't have shared so much with her, regardless of how relaxed I felt in her presence. I needed to stay more aware of what I shared. Nothing, and no one, could get in the way of my mission.

"How long has passed since you were turned?"

Wait, what! That's what she had to say after what I admitted...? How odd.

Her question caught me off guard, though, and I spluttered as I tried to recall the timing. "Uhm, only...uh, I'm not really sure what time it is right now. I also passed out for a little bit, but I know for sure I was turned after two in the morning."

Her breath caught as her eyes widened. "You

were turned only hours ago? How is it even possible for you to have control of your mind right now? Fledglings are often under supervision for weeks, if not months, until they are able to control their urges. It is imperative for you to be with those who can help you in the case that it does overcome you. At the Academy, we can teach you how to survive and learn the skills you will need as a vampire. You shouldn't be alone, not now."

She took a few steps closer to me, closing the distance between us in seconds. My fist tightened at my sides as her scent grew stronger, beckoning me. Holding my breath, I attempted to staunch the flow of the smell as my body shivered in delight at the mere thought of drinking from her.

"If I didn't see the reds of your eyes and the tips of your fangs peaking out myself, I would never have guessed," she admitted as she studied me. Her tone held a hint of awe.

But that couldn't be right, surely.

When she reached out to grab my hands, squeezing as she glanced down at me with a tenderness I didn't deserve, her awe was apparent. "Your eyes tell me many things about you, but none of them deserve you being called a monster. I see immense grief and self-hatred above all else. Let me assure you, of all the true monsters I've met, not one grieves or hates themselves for what they've done."

I simply blinked at her, struggling to process how she could look at a woman, stained with blood and admitting her wrong-doing, and be so kind. Sure, she mentioned being from Divinus as a goddess, but I was starting to wonder if she might actually have angel blood.

Ripping my hands from hers as her words soothed my jagged, broken soul, I stepped back a few feet, unwilling to accept the kindness she was bestowing upon me. I needed to breathe without her in my space and shifted the topic back to what was truly important. "What would you expect of me *if* I attended your school?"

I couldn't handle her kindness right now. It only served to muddle my thoughts, and I needed to focus.

Her lips thinned with her understanding, but she nodded after a short moment. The tension lining my shoulders released, relief flooding my being when she didn't push the subject of my worth.

"We are home to supernatural creatures who hone their skills over a four year period with us. Once they graduate, they are often offered highly sought after positions in Praeditus."

Now that I could work with. Maybe I could find a position close to Dracula. It might be a more long term plan than I initially hoped for, but it would be the path with the highest probability of success.

Cocking my head to the side, I mulled over that *potential* plan before asking, "What positions are available to..." I faltered, the word sounding vile enough in my head to give my pause. With a grimace, I forced out the remaining word, "Vampires?"

With hands clasped before her, she hummed in excitement. "Each sector of our academy hosts different species of paranormal creatures, with each focusing on different classes that are vital to their kind. For vampires, with their enhanced physical attributes and cunning minds, many of the positions available are as guards to important leaders in Praeditus or on task force teams that protect their city. However, there are positions for diplomats and strategists who work directly with leaders as well."

That was fucking perfect. It felt like I was being offered exactly what I needed on a shiny, silver platter.

Forgetting any semblance of playing it cool, I quickly asked, "What about a position with Dracula?"

Her eyes narrowed, and she observed me fidgeting for a silent moment before letting out a laugh. Tension melted from my body as she shook her head, mirth clear in her bright blue eyes, and responded, “Oh, sweet child, that man has never let anyone onto his board from our school. He is the most private leader in Praeditus, which, if you knew the fae queen in Natura, you would know that’s saying a lot.”

Not knowing who the fae queen was, I breezed past her joke with a single-minded focus. “So what you’re saying is that there are positions within Sanguis with the vampires as a member of a task force but not directly to advise or guard Dracula? I don’t want to go to another territory.”

“Yes,” she assured me, “there are absolutely positions that would allow you to remain with your kind in Sanguis.”

Your kind.

She prattled on, unaware of how deeply those two words cut. “From what I understand, the vampires could desperately use more task force members to help them keep their booming population in line. The slayers can only do so much.”

It was like a knife to the gut, thinking about crossing lines like this. Would I have to fight slayers at some point if I went down this path? I couldn't do that. My stomach turned as I thought of the way she spoke about the vampires trying to keep their kind in line humanized them. There was no way they cared like that. Otherwise, our job as Slayers wouldn't exist.

Even with my stomach turning and my mind rejecting the humanization of my sworn enemies, attending the academy still seemed like my best option for now. I'd figure out the rest as I went.

"Okay," I agreed, "I'll go to Dark Imaginarium Academy with you. I likely won't have the money to pay tuition fees, though. Not now."

A place like Dark Imaginarium Academy had to be expensive. In the past, I could have afforded the academy without question. In my new position, accessing the Van Helsing wealth simply wasn't an option.

Her tinkling laugh floated through the air as she turned and gestured toward the portal. "Our academy is not funded by tuition. Our students are admitted on their own merit, not on their financial status."

My head reared in shock, and a begrudging respect for the academy sprouted within me. That's how it should be. A person's worth wasn't tied to their wealth, but many territories and planes didn't operate with that mindset.

Estrid stepped toward the portal before pausing and glancing over her shoulder at me. Taking a deep breath, I followed her to the portal. "What's your name, dear?"

I stumbled over my feet, stopping with a wide-eyed glance at the question. It should've been an answer that was as easy as breathing to give. But I suddenly wasn't sure that sharing my family name was a good idea. Would it be a detriment to my mission?

Floundering to try to come up with a different last name, I found that nothing came to mind. Steadfast, my mind refused to part with who I was. It was as I always said, I would be who I was until death came to take me.

I could absolutely flip this to seem as if I defected from the slayer cause of my own free will. Perhaps that would even earn me respect, and it would certainly keep me from tangling myself in a web of lies if I had to come up with an identity of someone from Sanguis with the vampires.

Either way was a gamble, especially if I was being targeted by Dracula himself. In my gut, admitting who I truly was felt like the best option. All I could do was hope the decision didn't come back to bite me in the ass. The damn bite of loyalty to my family name.

Raising my chin up, I looked Estrid in the eyes as I announced, "I'm Alina Van Helsing."

4

ALINA

"A Van Helsing?" she parroted before shaking her head in disbelief. "I suppose that would explain why I found you in the slayer's territory. It seems we have much to discuss."

I refrained from commenting, assuming it was best for her to lead the conversation so I could steer it where I wanted with my answers. Now that I understood this route was the best option for me, I didn't want to give her the opportunity to think I was hiding anything of note. I couldn't jeopardize this opportunity. I assumed plotting to use the skills and power this academy could provide me to kill a leader of a territory would put my admission to the place at risk.

Motioning to the portal, she beckoned for me to

go first. With one last glance over my shoulder, I said goodbye to the life I had taken for granted. The life I'd complained about having hours ago. I'd give anything to have it back now, but the time had come to accept that I was living with the consequences of my actions.

I'd compartmentalize my emotions as I had been trained to do, in order to complete this mission. Never again would my emotions be the cause of my failure.

Stepping through the swirling air, I closed my eyes and held my breath, feeling the pressure of traveling through space pressing down onto me uncomfortably until I felt my feet land on the other side.

Taking in the large wall that displayed what had to be at least one hundred books behind a dark, wooden desk, I stared at it in awe. I wanted to run my fingers along the spines of each and every book as I searched through them to see what her collection was made up of.

I whirled around as I heard a suctioning and popping noise, coming face to face with Estrid as she stepped through the portal as well right before it closed behind her. Waving her hand in front of my face, she smiled in triumph. "All clean again, and what a beautiful face you have."

I stood before her, dumbfounded. With magic, she'd cleaned the blood from my face with a wave of her hand. While kind of her, a part of me hated how easy it was to erase the proof of the atrocities I'd committed.

"Please, have a seat," she offered, motioning to the leather chair in front of the desk as she circled behind it and took her own seat.

The leather squeaked, giving away the fact that I began fidgeting at the second I settled. Sitting with my hands clasped in my lap, I twisted uncomfortably in the seat as I waited for her to dive into a line of questioning.

Flipping through some papers on her desk, she asked without looking up, "Will being amongst other vampires be an issue for you, given your upbringing?"

Will I want to run my blade through them? Eventually.

"No," I lied with ease, plastering a small smile on my face though it felt fake and dirty. "Considering the training I've been through, I actually think my upbringing will give me an advantage."

Meaning I'm going to kick all of their asses and enjoy it thoroughly.

She paused, the sound of rustling papers stilling as she looked up at me. "Should we hide where you're from? Even if you don't feel you have an issue being amongst the vampires, I cannot say the same grace will be given to you from the students when they find out you're from the most prestigious line of slayers."

My jaw unhinged slightly at the compassion in her voice and the depth of thought she was giving this situation. I was truly shocked that she would go to such lengths for me. That she was even thinking about how this transition could truly affect me if not handled correctly showed her character tremendously.

Shaking my head, I explained, "I'd like to be open about who I am and where I come from as long as it's on my terms to share that at the right time. Even if my classmates have a problem with my background, it won't change who I am."

This time, my words held nothing but the truth. I wasn't sure I had it within me to pull off being anyone other than my authentic self, but I had to be smart about when to reveal that information, otherwise it could really backfire.

"If only everyone shared that sentiment. I appreciate that you're applying that mindset to yourself and giving your peers the same respect, despite knowing it will likely be difficult."

As her words sank in, my stomach tightened and then fell. I heaved a deep breath and sucked my bottom lip into my mouth, nibbling on it as I considered the implication of her words. Guilt gnawed at my stomach as the kind woman stared at me, the pride reflecting in her eyes.

Shit, now I kind of felt bad. The realization that they were also who they were, even if I didn't agree with it, it hit a little different when I really considered that not all vampires were turned, some were also born. There was nothing they could do to change the situations and lineages they were born into.

But only a second later, I pictured Skye's staring at me, eyes clouding with fear, as she tried to escape my grasp, and the numb exterior slid back into place with ease. I wasn't here to be liked or to make friends. It didn't matter if I was accepted or not. I would focus on becoming a stand out student so I could receive the position I needed to enable my future plans. Anything else was a distraction I couldn't afford.

I would leave the vampires in peace if they offered me the same courtesy. They wouldn't become my targets unless they made themselves into an enemy during my stay here.

Tapping her fingers against the desk, Estrid looked momentarily lost in thought before shaking her head and dialing a number on the phone sitting on the corner of the desk. She pressed the speaker-phone button and leaned back in her chair as she let the line ring until the voicemail box of a woman named Victoria was accessed. Estrid's murmured annoyance over her need for two of Victoria left me feeling curious about the unknown woman's role here.

Estrid sighed her frustration before trying another number. Expecting Victoria on the other end of the line, I was shocked at the deep, rumbling voice that answered. He sounded less than enthused.

"What?"

Humor danced in Estrid's eyes as she met mine and winked. "Lincoln, don't sound so excited, dear. You might give yourself a heart attack."

The urge to chuckle almost outweighed my curiosity over the grumpy man on the other end of the line, but it was a different realization that struck me and left the laugh lodged in my throat. The more I was around Estrid, the more I liked her, and feeling anything other than grief and anger had felt impossible even an hour ago.

The man chuckled at her quip, and I found myself loving the sound of it. Inexplicably, I wanted to hear it again and again. I swear it came out of the phone and wrapped around me like a sensual hug, making my skin pebble with goosebumps.

His tone turned to a lighter, jovial one. “How can I assist you, Estrid?”

“I need you to come to my office immediately if possible. Bring some bags with you; we have a new student who likely needs to feed. I know it’s early, but Victoria hasn’t arrived to assist me yet.”

The silence was deafening as we waited for his response.

“Another late admission?” he asked, curiosity filling his tone. “Didn’t we just make an exception for one in the demon sector yesterday? Where are you finding these students?”

That piqued my interest, reminding me of Estrid joking about having to memorize her introduction speech when she appeared next to me earlier.

I didn’t want to believe that it was fate that brought Estrid to me. Because if I allowed myself to believe that, I'd have to accept that what happened this past night was fate, and that was utter bullshit. That wasn't fate, that was the decision of a power-hungry vampire and the folly of a girl who was so wrapped up in feeling sorry for herself that she lost sight of what was important when it mattered the most.

But I was curious about who else was brought here like I was. I was still piecing things together, but it seemed I wasn't likely to meet the other new student if they were in the demon sector, which was a shame. Maybe we could've been allies, bonding over the unusual way we were brought here. I suppose it was for the best, though. I'd watch my own back and trust in myself only if that's what it took to make it out of here intact, one step closer to my goals.

"You'll see when you get here," Estrid practically sang back before adding, "and don't forget the blood," before hanging up on the grumpy man.

At the second mention of blood, my hunger surged back to the forefront of my mind. I squeezed my hands tightly together in my lap, not wanting to seem like a damn animal who couldn't control herself.

"Sorry about his demeanor," Estrid offered with

a big smile, "he is the lead professor of the vampire sector because of his combat ability, not his people skills."

A small snort fell from my lips as I cracked a hint of a smile. "What do you mean? He sounds like a peach."

With perfect timing, the door swung open, revealing one of the most stunning men I'd ever seen. He leaned against the doorframe, relaxed as he quietly studied the scene in front of him. It was clear the man was confident in his presence and power, not feeling the need to prove himself to anything or anyone. There was no reason behind the draw I felt toward his simmering energy.

His quiet, powerful presence was attractive in a way I'd never experienced before. I hated when people felt the need to flaunt how powerful they were. Those with true power didn't need to prove it, rather relying on effortless confidence to convey the certainty they felt, knowing with certainty that they could handle anything that came their way.

His frame filled the door, and my eyes were drawn to his classically handsome face and the boredom portrayed there. The man was tall–he had to be near six foot three, maybe more. My mouth practically watered as I took in the dark, three-piece navy suit he wore like a badge of honor. There was just something about a man in a suit...The quiet confidence he exuded only made me want to rip the suit off, but only after I'd properly stared enough to create a mental picture.

As my eyes traveled up, landing on his face, I schooled my features to hide my shock at finding him examining me in the same manner. His hazel eyes practically glowed, matching his dark, wavy hair. It was short and well groomed, with lighter bronze streaks flowing through it perfectly.

When our gazes locked, there was an immediate tension that radiated between us as something within me felt as if it were battling him for dominance. I'd never experienced anything like it before. I refused to back down from the challenge in his eyes, feeling my brows pull together slightly as I sent the same energy back to him.

"Is this the new student?" he asked, his rumbling tone spreading through the room with an authority that hit me deep in my core. I shifted in my seat, clenching my thighs together tightly.

I heard the creak of Estrid's chair as she stood up, but I refused to break eye contact. I squared my shoulders as her voice wafted from behind me, "Yes, this is Alina Van Helsing, the newest member of our vampire sector's incoming class."

At the mention of my name, his mouth fell open a fraction and his eyes darted between me and Estrid several times. Fighting the urge to smirk at my victory, I kept my cool mask of indifference in place instead. Worry ate at my gut as I waited to see his real reaction to my name. For some reason, I didn't want him to look at me differently because of my lineage.

"A Van Helsing? Are you out of your damn mind, Estrid?" he practically yelled, springing his perch against the door frame to walk closer to the head-mistress. "Why would I *ever* train a slayer?"

He spat the last word with such disgust, it was impossible for me to contain my emotions. I wouldn't let him insult me or my family, regardless of my mission. Leaping to my feet, I slid between him and the desk, shoving a finger into his chest. "Don't you dare disrespect slayers. They are the most honorable people on any plane of existence."

The hazel color of his eyes began to change, shifting until bright red eyes stared back at me. I always found it fascinating, seeing the shift in eye color that indicated the bloodhaze was taking over a vampire. Bloodhaze was different from bloodlust, and the more dangerous of the two if you asked me. Bloodlust was hunger based and could be attributed to something as simple as a new vampire not understanding when to stop drinking from a host. A bloodhaze was more animalistic, based on extremely heightened emotions and feelings. They were quick to react, and it was never in a good manner in my experience. Still, I refused to back down or step away.

Stooping until we were eye to eye, he smiled, the sight sarcastic and void of any sort of warmth. His fangs lengthened as he hissed, "You have no idea the number of senseless deaths the slayers have doled out."

As I opened my mouth to argue, Estrid clapped once, loudly. Her tone was sharp as she yelled, "Back away from one another, now! I will not have my new student feeling endangered, nor will I allow any of my faculty to be harmed either."

Shit, I thought as I fell back a step. I really needed to control myself in front of the woman who single-handedly determined whether I could stay here.

Taking another begrudging step back, I let my eyes move from him to Estrid as I bowed my head. "I apologize, headmistress. I'll work on not allowing myself to be riled so easily."

It was a kiss ass move, but I wasn't above it. I couldn't be above it. I needed her, and I needed the academy.

Truthfully, I wasn't sorry in the fucking slightest for my outburst. In fact, I would've happily called Devorare to me then and there to settle the fight between us. Instead, I forced my simmering rage down, alongside my hunger, as I sat down, steadfastly refusing to look at the gorgeous man who riled me faster than anyone I'd met before.

Bastard.

From the corner of my eye, I watched him unbutton his jacket and reach inside of a pocket before two dark crimson bags flew through the air and landed in my lap. "Eat up, *fledgling*. Your eyes show you haven't passed the initial stage of bloodlust yet."

On its own, that sentence probably would have never offended me, but the emphasis on fledgling really grinded my gears. He said it with such irreverence, it was impossible to feel that he viewed me as less than him. And this was the same vampire who just let his own emotion spur on his bloodhaze. Fucking hypocrite.

My throat clenched, distracting me from my distaste for him as my eyes landed on the bags of blood. Grimacing at the thought of drinking it, I tried to talk myself into it.

Just close your eyes and pretend, Alina.

Then he had to go and bark out a laugh, "Are you kidding me? I'm supposed to train her when she hasn't even accepted who she is enough to drink animal blood?"

Animal blood? That, at least, made me feel slightly better about the source.

He prattled on, throwing his hands in the air, "Give me a fucking break, Estrid. She's too soft for this school and the other students in our sector. She won't survive a week."

My chest rose and fell rapidly as I crossed the threshold of insults I could reasonably sit here and take without responding. I wasn't weak, and I wouldn't be bullied out of this school. I was a Van Helsing, and I'd prove that my skills were not something to turn his nose up at.

I'd prove that I was the strongest student here, and if it turned out I wasn't, I'd work my fucking ass off until it was a blatant fact.

The first step was drinking this damn blood so I didn't lose control.

Knowing it was animal blood tamped down the disgust slightly, but I still had to force myself to rip the cap off the first bag and quickly suck it down before repeating it with the next. Trying to radiate a calm strength, I stood from the chair and walked to the trash can next to her desk, dropping the empty bags into them with a tight nod in her direction.

Turning on my heel, I offered Estrid a smile. "Thank you for offering me this opportunity. I won't waste it."

Lincoln's answering scoff pulled a sneer across my lips before I pressed them together tightly.

Estrid reached across the space, grabbing my hand and squeezing once before saying, "I know you won't, dear."

As she let my hand go, she turned to face Lincoln, scowling. "Figure out your issue and then eliminate it. This is a unique position, one that we've never been in before, but you will continue to show the grace and humility of the professor I know you to be, no matter who your student is. Do you understand me?"

It was so fucking hard to not raise a brow and smirk at the fucker as Estrid put him in his place. It felt so damn good to see him knocked down a peg. I bit down on my bottom lip to keep the smirk off my face, and I was pleasantly surprised to not feel fangs digging into the skin this time.

As I took stock of how my body was feeling, I didn't feel an ounce of hunger tugging at me. All I could assume was that the fangs had naturally retracted with that need gone.

This was so damn strange.

A mask of indifference slipped into place on Lincoln's face as he nodded his understanding. Estrid returned the nod before adding, "Show her to her new room, and ensure she's back here tomorrow morning to meet with Victoria to sort out her schedule. She needs to rest until then. She's had a really rough night, Lincoln."

Flashes of the night rose unbidden into my mind, assaulting me with images of viscera and gore, and I forced my attention on a random book on the shelves behind her, breathing deeply until I felt my control return.

Lincoln nodded his agreement before turning and walking toward the door. "Follow me," he commanded before stalking out of Estrid's office, not waiting for me to follow.

Estrid shot me two thumbs up and a big smile as I left, trailing after the broody fucker as we descended a few flights of stairs. Silence stretched between us as we descended the final stairs into what seemed to be a typical reception area. He didn't leave me much time to look around, pushing the front doors open with a bang as he stepped into the gleaming sunlight.

Truthfully, I was thankful that vampires not being able to be in the sun was a myth. I'd always been partial to the sun soaking into my skin, warming me up when I often felt so cold and detached inside. Feeling at peace with nature, like the warmth from the sun was thawing my heart, was something that I didn't think would ever change about me, regardless of the circumstances.

As soon as I crossed the threshold, he turned, pinning me to the wall of the building in a second flat. He glowered down at me as he pressed the bulk of his body against mine. The sudden pressure knocked the breath out of me, and my eyes narrowed with confusion as I stared up at him.

The fucker was fast. Much faster than I could track, even with my abilities. Maybe I really wouldn't be at the top of the food chain here.

"Don't expect to be treated differently than the other students. I will not protect you from them. They've all managed to test into this school–they weren't handed an admission without first proving their worth. This is the last chance I'm giving you to leave this school without an issue."

His intimidation tactics weren't working in the slightest. There was zero chance of him scaring me into giving up the only opportunity I had to complete my blood oath.

No one would rob me of this chance to lighten the weight I felt bearing down on my soul.

Staring up at him, I let the fire I felt burning in my veins reflect in my eyes as I hissed, "I have nowhere else to go if I can't make it work here. I will not let you, or anyone else here, take this from me. I will fight for my place here."

His eyes danced across my face as we stood in silence. Our bodies were so close our chests brushed against one another with each breath we took. Lincoln's own hot breath fanned across my face, smelling pleasantly minty. I hated that I liked the scent.

"Don't say I didn't warn you," he finally offered, backing away from me and turning to continue on our path.

He wasn't quick enough to hide the spark of intrigue I saw in his eyes, though.

5

LINCOLN

Glancing back to make sure she'd followed me through the gate to our sector of the academy, I saw her face for the first time without a guard up. She was devastatingly beautiful, her tan skin practically glowing in the sun in contrast to her long, silver hair. Her plush lips taunted me, making me ache with the need to feel them wrapped around my cock. The leather outfit she wore accented her curves. Unfortunately, it was a stark reminder of the dumb fucking wardrobes slayers were always in.

Which was just another reminder of the chasm that would always separate us. And for good reason.

I pushed away thoughts of our differences and focused my attention on her appearance once more.

If she knew I was watching, I had no doubt the wall would slam back up in an instant. But for this brief moment, I let myself take in her expressive wonder and commit it to memory.

Soon enough, she'd be out of this school, and my life, forever. If nothing else, I'd make sure she was expelled simply by being up her fucking ass about following every rule we had. We had a policy at the academy that if you had more than three misdemeanors in a semester, you were out. The spaces at this school were limited, and we expected the best out of each student that filled them.

She wouldn't make it out alive if I didn't get her kicked out. My students were the best of our kind, both in terms of physical abilities and their cunningness. They would chew her up and spit her out, especially Andrei. He'd flay her skin open if he thought she was even the slightest threat to his top spot at the academy. He had some serious daddy issues to work through, but I understood it. The pressure he was under with his dad being a Bishop of Dracula's board was insurmountable. Excellence was an understatement of what was expected from the child of a board member.

I had tested her abilities when I'd pinned her to the exterior of the administration building, hoping that maybe she'd surprise me. Instead, I'd found her severely lacking. With her total lack of defense, she would've been dead if that's what I'd wanted.

It reaffirmed my decision to have her removed, forcibly if necessary.

"You'll be provided everything you need in your dorm room," I informed her, pulling her attention away from the sights of the grounds as we walked. I was in no way surprised as her mask slid back into place.

As we walked up the black metal staircase of the dorm house, I continued, "All students reside within this building, and each have their own room. The bottom level has a cafeteria to satiate hunger at any hour. I'd advise you to familiarize yourself with it, so you don't fuck up and drain someone and get yourself expelled."

It was flippant advice because I was going to get her expelled regardless, but for now, I had a role to play as her professor. I didn't want to bring Estrid's wrath down upon me if it was too blatantly obvious what I was trying to do. It was obvious these last minute additions to the Academy were special to the Headmistress. Shock wasn't a strong enough word to convey how I felt about Alexandra's arrival yesterday, followed by Alina's today. The last time Estrid had felt a pull toward a student that needed her was easily a decade ago, and now we'd had two in two days? Strange things were happening.

Alina's footsteps came to a halt behind me, and I glanced over my shoulder, annoyance gnawing at my gut, to see why. Her skin had paled considerably, and she seemed completely zoned out, like her brain had gone to another plane and left her body behind. She stood stock still, body stiff as if she were paralyzed.

I whipped my head around, scanning the first floor to try to gauge whether anyone else was here who could do this to her. An annoyed growl tore through my throat when I realized we were alone. It didn't mean that there wasn't someone behind this still. A witch could easily do this from afar.

I felt like I'd lost all control of myself as I quickly descended the few steps between us, running the back of my fingers against the soft skin of her cheek. "Alina, what's wrong?"

I shouldn't have touched her.

I shouldn't have shown any sign of tenderness.

But fuck, I couldn't help myself.

Before Estrid dropped the bomb that she was a slayer, I'd felt a pull toward her I'd never experienced before. There was something damaged within her, something beyond repair. It practically oozed from her as our gazes met for the first time in Estrid's office. I wanted to pull her into my embrace then and promise to protect her from the world, but the most intriguing part of her was that I could tell without a doubt that she didn't want someone else to protect her. No, she was a fighter.

It made my cock hard instantly, seeing her unwillingness to back down from me.

And then it had gone soft again just as quickly when Estrid dropped the bomb of her true identity. It was a true fucking shame, but it was probably for the best considering I was her professor. Within our code of ethics, it was strictly prohibited to have relations with our students. That wasn't to say some professors hadn't crossed the line before, especially Helen of the Demi-god sector, but I'd never once found the desire to push that boundary myself.

I'd been at the academy with Estrid from the very beginning, and as such, had always felt a strong sense of loyalty to it and her. What we offered here was the truly magnificent opportunity for these young adults to exceed the constraints of the lives they were born into.

Pulling myself back into the urgency of the moment, I studied Alina, finding that there was no fire in her eyes. My Spitfire was gone, and in her place was someone buried under immense pain, someone trapped with no way out. It seemed as if she was experiencing a waking nightmare.

If someone wasn't using magic on her, was there something I'd said to trigger this response from her? My mind whirled as I thought back to warning her not to accidentally drain someone. Was that it? Had she already drained someone?

It would make sense. Even though she seemed to have superior control for her age, she *was* still a fledgling. Accidentally draining a person wasn't uncommon, and it would explain why she'd looked at the blood bags with disgust when I'd tossed them in her lap.

Suddenly she snapped out of it, sucking in a sharp breath and blinking rapidly at my chest before glancing up at me.

It felt like time stopped as my fingers stilled on her face. For just a moment, neither of us wore the masks we'd donned earlier. Could I really send her away now? Would that take away the sudden and compelling fixation I felt toward her?

Then she opened her mouth, breaking the spell as she shifted back into being a little fucking brat once more. "Don't touch me."

Fuck, what was I doing? She might have been of a legal age, but compared to myself, she was nothing more than an insolent child. Not to mention she was a fucking slayer. And a student on top of all of it.

There were so many damn reasons that I needed to keep a distance. And there were about a thousand more reasons that I needed to focus my attention on ensuring she was expelled as quickly as possible.

Dropping my hand as if she'd burned me and curling my lip in disgust, I turned back to ascend the stairs.

It was in my nature to want to hurt her, yet I hated the idea of her in pain. Even more, I hated the thought of my students hurting her. It was the reason I needed her gone. Well, one of the main ones.

Slayers deserved to pay. Afterall, they were the ones who slaughtered my parents with abandon, not caring that they'd brought me to the human plane of Ordinarius at a young age to offer me a better future. They'd wanted a fresh start away from the political games that plagued Sanguis. My father was a high-ranking vampire, renowned as a Knight on Dracula's chessboard, but it was a dangerous board to be on and my parents wanted out.

Somehow they'd been outed a month into our

stay with the humans, and the slayers were called in. I'd been just a boy at the time, out delivering milk bottles for a meager income to try to help us afford to live in this new society. When I returned home, I found their heads severed. In a state of panic, I located the portal that traveled directly from Sanguis to here that resided within Dracula's castle. Only those on his board knew where to locate the portal, and I'd made sure to remember it when we'd come through in Ordinarius.

I ran back to the only people I thought could help me. I'd pleaded with the guards to help me, and they'd scoffed in my face instead, telling me my parents got what they deserved for deserting our kind. With nowhere to go, they'd placed me into the care of the government, sending me to combat school and providing me a cot within an orphanage with the other children who happened to fall into the same position.

We'd simply been trying to blend in, to live in peace, and slayers stole everything from us.

Hell, it was why I'd come to the academy to begin with. All I knew was living and breathing combat and strategy, with no family to care for me. Schooling had become my life, and when Estrid approached me with the offer of a sizable salary, I'd accepted eagerly. It allowed me to stay far away from the slayers, and the job held me to a routine in life that I'd grown comfortable with.

"Tell anyone I was kind to you, and I'll ensure you're in detention every waking second outside of your classes," I warned her, my voice full of venom.

Her steps resumed, following me as we reached the third floor where the female students resided. The male students were assigned to the second floor, and teachers were left with the fourth.

A scoff rang out as she countered, "As if I want anyone here thinking I'm getting special treatment. When I have the top spot at this school, I want there to be no doubt in anyone's mind that I fucking earned it and deserve the position I want after this."

The passion with which she said that made me believe that, at some level, she truly wanted this. It was admirable, even for a slayer. I thought back to her saying she'd have nowhere to go if she didn't stay here. For the briefest moment, I felt a twinge of guilt at the thought of ensuring her expulsion, but it was for the best. No amount of fire burning within her could prepare her for what was to come on Monday when classes began. She'd learn that quickly enough, hopefully changing her tune.

Taking a left, I brought her to the last dorm

available in the hallway. Fate was a cruel-hearted bitch for ensuring this thorn in my side would be living in the room directly beneath mine. Relief speared through my gut at the thought of at least being able to hear if anyone broke into her dorm and attempted to harm her, though. I would have to ensure she was monitored closely until she was removed from the premises.

I was simply doing my duty as her professor, nothing more.

Keep telling yourself that, Lincoln.

My mind was a swirling mess of contradictions. Needing my space to clear my head, I opened the door and gestured for her to go in. "This is your room. The other students will arrive tomorrow, and classes begin on Monday. Feel free to go to the cafeteria at any point but don't leave our sector. Students from different sectors are not allowed to mingle unless at a supervised Academic event."

The restriction had never stopped the students from having a party every damn first Monday of the school year, though. We let it slide, allowing them to get it out of their systems early. Breaking the rules helped them feel accomplished. The hangovers they suffered the next day was all the victory the faculty and staff needed. Was it flawed?

Maybe, but it was truly best for all parties involved.

We supervised from the shadows, anyway. I was a glorified adult babysitter that first Monday. Though sometimes it felt like the babysitters club extended beyond the party.

As she brushed by me, my eyes rolled back as I breathed in her scent. It was something woodsy mixed with leather, and it was an intoxicating combination that suited her perfectly. Wild and untamed, like the forest on the edge of a storm.

"Okay, bye," she snapped, tossing her long hair over her shoulder as she surveyed the small room, keeping her back to me the entire time.

My hand tightened around the doorknob, rage settling in my gut at her dismissive attitude. The metal warped, twisting and cracking beneath my strength. Taking a deep breath, I forced myself to let go of it, letting my hand fall to my side.

What I wouldn't give to wrap my hand around her throat, making her beg for air to be able to sass me back. Maybe that's what she needed, someone to take away the opportunity to talk back. I could do that for her. Desire burned in my veins as I thought about backing her against the wall, making her gasp for air as my fingers tightened around her throat.

The thought of then shoving her to her knees and filling her throat with my cock was intoxicating. I knew her eyes would flash with hatred as I did it, and I loved the thought of it. I wanted that hatred because it would help keep my disgust for her kind at the forefront of my mind. But I also knew that my Spitfire loved a challenge, so she wouldn't back down when I forced her to gag on my cock. I'd watch the tears run down her face and let my cum spill down her throat.

"Why are you standing there, staring at me like a fucking creep?"

Her voice snapped me out of the day dream I'd fallen into, and I growled at her before turning around and racing up the stairs to find my room. I had to figure out how to get a fucking grip on myself when I was around her. The desire for her was unacceptable on so many levels.

Slamming my door shut behind me, I paced the dark, hardwood floors before pouring myself a stiff drink at my wet bar. I sighed around the alcohol burning pleasantly down my throat before it settled in my chest. With a deep breath, I closed my eyes and attempted to center myself.

Yet somehow, my cock still twitched in my pants, and the image of her on her knees for me came roaring back. What I needed was a cold fucking shower.

Heading to the ensuite with the intention to get rid of this hard-on one way or another, I faltered when my heightened hearing picked up a sniffling noise followed by a loud, hiccuping breath coming from beneath me.

Alina was crying.

The strong woman who oozed a 'don't fuck with me attitude' and acted like it was her versus the world was sobbing, the sound dragging me to a stop. It was such a jarring juxtaposition to the snarky woman who'd snapped at me just minutes ago that I stood there for a moment, disbelief roiling through me in churning waves.

I took an involuntary step in the direction of the door, the need to see her, to comfort her overwhelming my senses. Thankfully the madness passed as my mind caught back up, preventing me from crossing that boundary again.

Get a fucking grip, I thought to myself.

Alina had made it abundantly clear that she didn't want my concern. Beyond that, I needed to remember not only my job, but my overall goal with her as well. As shitty as it sounded, maybe if she was miserable enough, she'd leave of her own accord.

Surely, she could figure out her shit on her own. We all had our own demons to fight.

It *should* have been that simple.

So then why did I sit on my bed, listening to her cry until I was sure she'd fallen asleep?

Why did I feel like I was in physical pain, letting her go through it alone?

Throwing my empty glass at the wall when my frustrations welled to an unmanageable level, I relished in the sound of the shattering glass, breaking me from the trance I had fallen into.

I was so fucked.

6

ALINA

A pounding on the door pulled me from sleep, and I groaned before burying my face into my pillow. It couldn't seriously be time to face the world again.

Despite having all day and night to rest, I still felt on the knife's edge of exhaustion. Physically and mentally, I was drained. I thought I'd managed to isolate my pesky emotions and tuck them away, but when Lincoln made that comment about not fucking up and draining someone...The wound was too fresh to ignore, and I was transported back to that moment with Skye. I barely managed to pull myself out of the memory and make it to my room before I dropped to my knees and fell to pieces the moment I shut the door.

It was easier to stave off the pain when I wasn't alone. Being trapped within the four walls of this new, unfamiliar place while seeing the blood of my mom and Skye dried on my leathers in a mirror...it was too much. Even for someone who had been trained to separate themselves from their emotions. Or maybe I was just that big of a failure as a slayer. I couldn't keep my guard up, and I couldn't isolate my emotions.

So, instead of isolating, I'd let it all out. If I was going to blaze down this path, I couldn't afford to let myself slip up in front of the vampires like I'd done on that staircase with Lincoln. I had left myself exposed to an attack, just like I had with my mom after I'd been forced to drive my sword through her heart. It felt like like no matter my intentions, I just kept fucking up.

No more. I would no longer let the atrocities of that night distract me from the one reason I had to continue in this life.

Sure, I'd said that before, but dammit, I really meant it now.

I wouldn't be able to rise to the top if I was barely controlling my grief and drowning in my sorrows. So I let the tears fall, and I wallowed in self-pity until sleep claimed me.

While trying to rest through the day, I woke up time and again in a fright, remembering horrid moments from the night before. Each time, all I could think was that I had to come to terms with the fact that the memories weren't just a horrible nightmare—this was my new reality. The beheaded bodies, the staked heads, the pain and fear in Skye's eyes, the crimson blood of my family that stained my home. Accepting that I would never be welcomed into our ancestral resting place with my family. All of it, while nightmarish, was real now.

"Alina, hurry up," Lincoln grumbled from the other side of my door. "We have an appointment with Victoria this morning to get your schedule. I don't have time to babysit you all day."

Rolling my eyes, I lifted my middle finger to flick off the door. He was so damn aggravating. On more than one occasion, I found myself blaming him for my tears. When I'd come out of my daze on the steps to the dormitory, he'd been looking down at me with tenderness, and the soft way his fingers brushed my cheek... It had almost been my undoing. I'd wanted to fall into his arms and allow myself to be comforted by him as I let go of all my grief and anger. I wanted to be held and reassured that everything would be okay.

But everything wasn't okay, and confiding in that asshole wasn't an option. So, I'd forced myself to be as dismissive as possible of him in the hope that he would leave me in peace before my tenuous grip on my control slipped.

Flinging the covers off of me, I stood, stretching my arms above my head as I tried to figure out what I was supposed to wear. The leathers I'd stripped off in favor of bathing away my sweat, and horror, and guilt in the middle of the night were not an option. They might have been cleaned by Estrid's magic, but no amount of magic could clean away the sins that had soaked into those leathers. I swept my gaze around the room at a temporary loss.

The room itself was actually quite charming if you were one for a dark-broody vibe, which I absolutely was. The walls were a light grey, contrasting the dark, almost black, hardwood floors and matching the exposed wood beams on the ceiling.

Padding over to the black armoire, I yanked the doors open and let out a horrified shriek. There was a boutique's worth of fucking prep school looking bullshit outfits. I was assaulted with a variety of black, red, plaid, and white in the form of pants, skirts, and blazers.

The door burst open behind me, and Lincoln burst into the room yelling, "What's wrong?"

Turning around and pointing my finger in the direction of the offensive outfits, I asked, "Do you seriously think I'd ever be caught dead wearing that shit? It strips all individual identity from students, limiting them from self-expression and puts them into neat little boxes of conformity!"

For a long, silent moment, he stared at me, jaw agape. I arched a brow in his dumbfounded direction, challenging him to really stand there and tell me I was wrong. After a quiet beat passed between us, an amused look settled over his face. Lincoln smirked, leaning against the wall by the door like he owned the place as he crossed his arms over his chest. "And you think the fact that so many slayers wear black leather outfits allows for individual identity? Interesting, tell me more."

Motherfucker. That condescending tone alone would be the reason I got kicked out of this school.

My lips thinned as I thought about how many slayers traditionally opted for black leathers and muttered, "We don't have to wear that. I just happened to love it, okay...and so do some other slayers. It's badass."

A smug as fuck look settled over his stupidly

handsome face as he kicked off the wall, running his fingers through his annoyingly shiny hair. He started toward the door, pausing to call out, "It doesn't matter what you wear, Alina. As long as you wear something."

It seemed very unlike him to give in so easily, and I could feel my face screwing up in confusion. I didn't know the man very well, but the lack of argument seemed more than a smidge out of character. Dismissing the thought, I shrugged, deciding to take the win. I could use the boost to my confidence today.

Alina- 1.

Lincoln- 0.

Humming happily, I turned back to the armoire, hoping to find the least hideous outfit possible amongst the travesty pleats and starched cotton, but the blood drained from my face as I caught sight of myself in the floor-length mirror in the corner.

I was naked.

"Fuck!" I screeched, realizing now why he'd stared at me in shock before settling in against the wall for a show. Stomping over to my door, I slammed it shut, but not before his laughter rang through the hallway. The brassy timbre of his laugh only served to piss me off further.

Grumbling under my breath about how he was a fucking ass muncher, I yanked a black pair of jeans out from a shelf and a beige bra along with a plain white shirt. It wasn't my preference, but I was grateful for the alternative to the hideous uniform.

Clothing didn't distract me for long. Eventually, my thoughts turned back to that infuriating man. He was a damn professor. Shouldn't he have apologized and left immediately? Instead, he lounged around like he was right at home. And he had the audacity to make a mockery of my situation. The longer I was around him, the more I believed Estrid assigned him to me to test my patience and get under my skin before I was immersed in classrooms full of vampires.

Truly, if I could survive Lincoln's insufferable attitude, I'd be golden with everyone else. He just had this uncanny ability to make me want to strangle him. An incredibly unfortunate side effect he was having on me was making me want a few other things that I absolutely couldn't allow myself to dwell on...much.

The tension between us was palpable, and I found myself wondering whether I was the only one thinking how explosive it would be if we let the tension transfer to a more intimate moment.

The memory of him stroking my face on the steps followed by staring at me like he wanted to snack on me once I was in my room resurfaced, and I could feel heat blossoming in my core at the memory of his eyes on my skin. He hated me one minute, cared about my well-being in another, and then eyed me like a piece of meat to devour whole at the end. His ever-evolving moods were giving me whiplash.

Once dressed, I took a deep breath, trying to expel him from my mind as I blew it out.

He's your professor, Alina. He hates you, and you hate him. He is a vampire, and you are a slayer.

If only those motivators were enough to make my traitorous mind stop imagining digging my long nails into his back as he fucked me wildly, drawing blood from him and making him hiss in pain-tinged pleasure. I just knew he'd like it rough, and I'd more than give him a challenge in that regard. If I was being honest with myself, I was beginning to enjoy these interactions with the moody bastard.

Today I'd awoken with a sense of...Well, I wasn't sure how to describe it exactly. But I was left feeling detached and emotionless. It was like with each tear was a release of my grief, and that I had mourned, giving up who I was and the life I always thought I'd have. The tether to that version of me was fraying thinner as I detached myself from who I was.

Maybe that was why, deep down, I loved the power struggle between Lincoln and myself. It felt forbidden and dangerous in a way that only made me want it more. I wanted to be burned by it. The rush of the hate and adrenaline from our encounters felt like a life preserver, keeping me afloat and feeling anything at all when it would be all too easy to go completely numb instead.

But was allowing myself to feel that hate a mistake? Perhaps losing myself to the emotionless pit of my soul was the best way to achieve my goal. Every decision would be based in logic, detached from emotions threatening to change my path.

I yanked on a pair of boots I found at the bottom of the armoire, huffing a breath of frustration as thoughts of Lincoln invaded my mind again. Standing, I glanced at my reflection in the mirror before running my fingers through my hair and calling it a day. Heading out the door, I steadfastly ignored Lincoln, who leaned against the wall opposite my door with a smirk pulling his lips up at the corners. Grinding my teeth in an effort to not make a smartass comment to him, I brushed past him toward the stairs.

"Come now, Alina," he called out, his voice sounding from close behind me. "You talk about the freedom of self-expression through clothing and then wear black jeans and a white shirt. How bland."

This fucking dude.

A frustrated groan bubbled from my throat, and I couldn't contain the frustrated sound as I turned on my heel and glowered. "Your opinion of how I look doesn't matter, you fucking pervert."

To be fair, I didn't care that he'd seen me naked. I was comfortable in my skin, which is why it was so easy for me to forget I wasn't wearing clothes when he burst in, but I hated how I immediately cared whether he liked what he saw. It left me open to a vulnerable and emotional side of myself, a side that every woman could relate to. A side that thrived on the fear of not being good enough. I couldn't think of a time when I'd given a shit about what a man thought about me, and it rattled me to realize that I did care what Lincoln thought about me.

His head tipped back, the same rumbling laugh I'd heard over the phone in Estrid's office spilling from his lips. He looked like a completely different man at that moment, and I found myself staring in appreciation at this care free version of him. Even his outfit was dressed down from the three-piece I'd seen him in the day before. Today, he wore black dress pants and a white dress shirt–I hated how enticing it was to see him so immaculately put together.

Brushing past me, he countered, "Good, because you don't want to know my opinion on the matter."

Not waiting for my response, he began his descent of the stairs. My face burned as I ran my tongue along my teeth. I nodded my head as I stared after him, internalizing the comment that made my stomach burn with inexplicable shame. How had I been rejected without even trying?

"Come, Alina," he called, treating me like a fucking dog that needed to follow its master.

It was another stark reminder of why I needed to remember that it didn't matter what he thought of me. I needed to keep my guard up and look out for myself. If he wanted to fuck with me, I'd make sure I fucked him back ten times harder. While probably not a healthy mindset, it was what I needed right now. I was clinging to my sanity by the tips of my fingers, and he wasn't going to be the one to push me over the edge.

Taking a seat at the top of the stairs, I examined my black nails. I was meticulous about their care, ensuring the pointy coffin look stayed intact. A shit-eating grin stretched over my face as I settled in to see how long it took him to realize I wasn't following.

He didn't make me wait long, turning back to glance up at me seconds later. As his lips thinned and his signature glower returned, replacing that annoying smirk he'd been wearing this morning, I relished in the change of his attitude. But it wasn't enough, not even in the slightest. I wanted to rile him, to make him feel as awkward and ashamed of the tension stretching between us as I felt.

"What are you doing?" he asked flippantly, tapping his foot against the step above him. "We have a meeting to get to. I don't have time for your antics."

Ahh, how easy it was to guess that he would go this route, trying to shame me into listening to him.

Returning my eyes to my nails, I nodded in understanding and muttered, "We sure do. A meeting that you were charged with getting me to. That would look pretty bad on you if you couldn't manage such a simple task, wouldn't it?"

My smile only grew as a deep growl emanated from him and he stomped up the stairs, closing the distance between us. Propping my elbows on my knees, I placed my chin in my hands and looked up at him innocently as he glared down at me. The promise of threatening energy crackled in the space between us.

"Problem?" I asked with a cheery tone, reveling in his deepening scowl.

"Get. Your. Ass. Up," he demanded, punctuating as his eyes began to shift into the light red tone that indicated a bloodhaze was forthcoming.

Excellent.

Pursing my lips and staring into the distance over his shoulder, I acted like I was thinking hard on his demand. I met his eyes, popping my lips with my answer. "Nope."

With that dismissive response, his eyes shifted to blood red, but before he could utter a word, I tacked on, "You should really control your emotions, someone could mistake you for a fledgling instead of a professor of this academy with the red eyes you're showing off right now."

I swore I would never forget this moment in my life. The thrill of shoving his own words back down his throat as an insult. It was an impossible high, and I desperately wanted to fuel it, to revel in the way it made me feel.

What I didn't expect was him running his

tongue over his bottom lip and bobbing his head a few times, as if in contemplation. With barely a flash of movement, his hand was around my throat and my back was flat against the floor. He straddled me, lowering his nose until it was inches from my own.

"You think you can just show up and call the shots, fledgling?"

Huffing a haughty breath through my nose, I arched my brow. His fingers weren't tight enough to restrict my air flow, which was his first mistake if he didn't want me to talk anymore. I answered honestly, "I know I don't call the shots around here, but I do know that you have a job to do, and I can either make that really fucking hard for you, or we can find a way to make this easier. The choice is up to you, *Professor*."

His chest rumbled against mine, and I felt his erection growing against me. It was good to know the fucker enjoyed this tension as much as I did.

My skin pebbled with goosebumps as he ran his thumb over a sensitive spot on my neck, forcing me to swallow around a lump in my throat as desire blossomed through me.

His voice dropped to a near whisper as he growled, "And what makes you think I'd ever choose the easy way, Spitfire? Why bother when the hard way is so much more fun?"

My eyes widened a fraction. It wasn't what I was banking on him saying in the fucking slightest. But I guess that's what made him challenging as hell to me. His fluctuating mood swings kept me on my damn toes.

As I opened my mouth to respond, he pressed his fingers into the sides of my throat, slowly increasing pressure. Fuck me sideways for loving the feeling of the control he took from me with that simple move. My eyes rolled back in my head as my body tingled with pleasure. I didn't ask him to stop, and he didn't give up, continuing to press harder until spots danced behind my eyes.

"Just as I thought," he murmured as I shifted my thighs to rub them together, aching to get any friction possible against my swollen clit.

I didn't give a shit about what he was saying right now. All I wanted was more of this feeling. Never before had someone managed to challenge me in a manner that I enjoyed. Finally, I'd found someone who I was sexually attracted to who wouldn't let me walk all over them. I'd been yearning for this sort of power struggle for so long

Of course, it had to be with a bloodsucker.

Releasing my neck, he shifted, grabbing my waist. Inertia dragged me along with him as he stood and tossed me over his shoulder like a rag doll. I was too confused about what just happened, and why I'd loved it so much, to fight off this caveman treatment.

As he covered the distance from our sector to the administration building with lightning speed, I tried really fucking hard to remember all the reasons I couldn't cross this line with him.

He was my professor.

He was a vampire.

He was a grade-a asshole.

But then he set me on my feet just outside of the doors and gripped my chin tightly. "Be a good girl, okay?"

All the reasons I couldn't cross that line with him went out the window with those five words.

Fuck, why did being called a good girl do it for me?

7

ALINA

Before I had the chance to respond, he was gone. I stood there, reeling until the door to the building cracked open and a soft voice called out, "Alina?"

Staring at the direction of our sector, I blinked rapidly, trying to force my brain to catch up to the present moment. Out of all the possibilities for how my bratty display could've gone, what occurred wasn't one I'd considered. Now I was left with desire coursing through my body, which wasn't exactly the best position to be in at the moment. I could feel the heat of a blush staining my cheeks, and as I took stock of my body, I quickly snapped my mouth shut.

Blegh, ew. I looked like a love sick puppy, which wasn't a good look for the record.

"He has that effect on many people," the same soft voice said, pulling me out of the haze of lust I had been stuck in.

Whipping my head to the source of those words, I found a tall, slender woman studying me with silver eyes. Raven colored hair fell in soft waves around her shoulders and chest. An air of easy confidence exuded from her, though not in a smug way. It reminded me of how Lincoln oozed power. It was easy to tell she was comfortable with who she was and wouldn't take anyone's shit.

As she smiled at me from the door, I took in the royal blue pencil skirt she'd paired with a black blouse and dangerously high stilettos. Damn her for encapsulating the perfect balance between business professional and a sensual woman. I was officially beyond jealous as I eyed my bland outfit in distaste. It was still better than a uniform, I quickly reminded myself.

Gesturing inside, she said, "Please, follow me to my office. I have a few appointments already planned with it being the official move-in day, and it will probably be a little hectic today. As we open each sector, students will arrive en masse."

It was hard to picture the expansive pavilion outside of the academic building teeming with supernatural creatures. It was like a ghost town now, and I found I enjoyed the silence. I guess all good things had to come to an end eventually.

With a tight smile, I followed her into the building and up the stairs to the second level of the building. The click of her heels only added to the confident energy I felt from her. What was it about the sound of heels echoing in a room that conveyed dominance? It was the ultimate power move.

At the top of the stairs, we turned right and continued in silence–the sound of her stilettos clicking against the floor was the only sound filling the eerily quiet level. We pulled to a stop outside a dark wooden door that had a name plate reading: Dr. Rythiu - Lead Counselor. I waited for her to open the door, but she stepped to the side and gestured toward it instead.

"Please press your finger into the door handle. It helps me verify my students by blood type and to assist me in our sessions. Normally, I would already be inside. This is how you will enter our appointments moving forward."

At her instructions, my face twisted in confusion before I turned my gaze on the odd, metal handle. The top piece clearly needed to be pressed down to release the latch to open the door, but there was a small indent within it that could accommodate a finger.

"Okay," I responded, drawing out the word, but I suppose unexpected and a little strange was par for the course at a magical academy. I mean, hell, my clothes somehow fit me perfectly, and I never had my measurements taken.

Fucking magic, man. It made an item as simple as a door handle something to suddenly be wary of.

Gripping the long handle with my fingers, I pressed my thumb into the top to engage the handle and open the door. Letting out a yelp as something bit into the pad of my thumb, I jumped back and swiped the tip of my nail into my palm, ready to call Devorare to me if needed.

I had expected something magical to happen–not for the door to inflict pain on me.

Instead of being attacked further by the door, a beep rang out before it popped open, revealing a perfectly normal looking office inside. Turning my attention to Victoria, I narrowed my eyes at the obvious way she was barely containing her laughter at my reaction.

"It's fucking weird, okay," I defended, straightening up and wiping my hand on my jeans to clear it of blood, seeing nowhere else to do so. Thankfully, my newfound rapid healing was coming in handy with the small wound. Already, it was sealing, leaving no trace of the small puncture.

The only response Victoria offered was a smirk before she pushed the door open further, leaving me trailing after her as she settled into the white chair behind her glass desk. It was a modern, yet minimalistic, room. Glancing at the chaise lounge to the right of the room, I wondered if this was supposed to be a *real* therapy session.

If so, she was going to be severely underwhelmed with my emotional capacity. I barely contained the laugh that threatened to bubble out of me at the thought of her asking me, "And how does that make you feel?" about what had happened in my life in the past twenty-four hours alone.

The truth was that it made me feel like a little bit of a sociopath to be able to shut down my feelings about the situation, locking them away after one good cry session. Did that make me a shitty person? I mean, it wasn't that I didn't care...It was more that I had been in a fight or flight, life changing moment, and I'd chosen to fight.

I could've fled and lived out the rest of my existence in the human plane, but I'd chosen vengeance. And in order to get it, I knew I needed ruthlessness, now more than ever. If you thought back in the history books, you didn't relate the ruthless victors of wars to being the same people who let their grief consume them, bringing them to their knees in front of the very people they swore to destroy. No, they took that pain and used it as their weapon in order to achieve victory.

You either let your grief and anger destroy you, or you employed them to destroy others. It seemed *that* simple to me now. I'd given myself a moment of weakness to grieve, and now it was time to navigate through what was next for me.

"Have a seat, Alina," she offered as she waved her arm toward the chaise in the corner. "You can either sit or lay down, whichever makes you most comfortable. I know it can seem odd at first."

I'd already been afraid of her door, I couldn't let her think I was afraid of a damn lounge chair at this point. And it wasn't like the chair was suddenly going to make me spill my darkest secrets to her...right? Shit, maybe it would, considering where we were.

Rolling my eyes at myself, I walked over and plopped down onto the grey suede chair as she pushed up from her chair and approached the door. There was some finality with the way the door clicked closed, and my stomach lurched. I shook my head, reminding myself I was being ridiculous as Victoria pressed a button on the side of the door. A small tube popped out, and from my position across the room, I could just make out the small amount of blood swirling inside of it.

Was that...my blood? From the handle pricking my thumb?

My head reared back as she brought the small tube to her mouth and tipped it back, allowing the blood to drop into her mouth. I saw the briefest hint of fangs peeking out with the move.

Oh, great. Another vampire.

The ounce of comfort I'd found in her presence flew out the door with that revelation. Clutching the arms of the chair, I tried to reason with myself. Perhaps I wasn't being fair to her. She seemed nice enough; but when growing up as a slayer and having seen utter destruction at the hands of vampires, my icy exterior came naturally to me when I was around one.

A gasp fell from my lips when her eye color changed to a light green as her attention turned to me. Suddenly, it felt like she was staring straight into my soul. Victoria took a few steps forward, leaning against the edge of her desk as she stared down at me, and I watched as her eyes shifted colors once more to a grey-blue.

As she stared down at me, the feeling of someone probing around inside of my chest blossomed, and I didn't appreciate the intrusion one bit. I narrowed my eyes at her, and I knew at that moment I was seconds away from getting up and walking out. But then her eyes shifted to pure obsidian as she inhaled a sharp breath, letting her mouth hang open slightly. It was creepy as hell to watch, looking like a demon had possessed her body or something.

Thankfully, she sagged back against the desk after a second, taking deep breaths and blinking rapidly.

"You good?" I asked, needing clarification to understand what the hell just happened after she sampled my blood.

I mean, I wasn't a genius, but it didn't seem...good.

Holding a hand up, she shook her head, as if asking for a minute to process it herself. After a beat of silence, she admitted, "That was a lot to take in. Estrid warned me that you likely suffered through a tough situation, but I never imagined this. She must not know the extent of what you've endured."

Alarm bells clanged loudly in my head, and I surged to my feet. "What did you do to me? I didn't give you permission to do whatever the hell that was with my blood."

Pinching the bridge of her nose and taking a deep breath before dropping her hands to her side, she pinned me with an unamused look before saying, "Please sit back down, Alina. I'll explain."

I stood, stuck somewhere between my curiosity and the urge to bolt. I glanced toward the door as Victoria rounded her desk and took her own seat before turning to me. She pulled a notebook and pen across the desk before resting it on top of her knees. I remained standing, staring at her in disbelief, before I began pacing in front of her desk like some sort of feral, caged animal.

Letting out a sigh, probably frustrated with my lack of cooperation, she began, "I'm a very rare type of vampire. Despite you being a Van Helsing, you might not have heard of my kind before. I'm an empath who can pick up on the moods of those around me without even tasting a drop of their blood. Usually, it's a dormant trait that runs in my family line. I happened to be one of the lucky ones."

The dark tone and scoffing laugh that accompanied her words said more about how she felt than her pinched brows and tensed shoulders did. It had to be a resourceful tool, being able to feel the emotions of those around you, but when I really thought about it, surely the ability could be overwhelming too.

I stopped dead in my tracks, staring at her in shock. How had I never heard of that ability before? Somewhere in my family line, you'd think someone would've heard about this. And if not my family, surely one of the other slayer houses should have uncovered this.

Tapping the end of her pen against the paper, she continued, "I'm often given our students who will face challenges during their attendance. Be it because of outside circumstances or what they are dealing with inside. Taking a drop of blood acts as a conduit, enhancing my powers to pinpoint the emotions to a degree that I can quite literally feel your emotions from your perspective."

I was fascinated by the power, but I couldn't afford for it to be used on me.

"I didn't consent to this," I growled, repeating myself. "This is a gross invasion of privacy."

For a moment she just stared at me, her eyes back to what I assumed was their natural silver state. I refused to look away as she asked, "What do you think I'm trying to do here, Alina? Do you think I'm trying to hurt you? To make your life more difficult? If so, please feel free to walk out that door, but just know that you cannot stay at this academy if you don't keep up with our sessions. You're a liability, and a danger, to our students and yourself in your current state."

The thought of being a liability hit a little too close to home, but rather than admitting the truth in her words, I deflected. There was no way I was going down that path right now.

My eyes practically bugged out of my head as I scoffed, "A liability? From what I gathered from Headmistress Estrid and Lincoln, I'm also in danger from the other students in my sector. But sure, let's just pretend like I'm the only issue here."

An odd, knowing look came over her before she stated, "It's Professor Aldea to his *students*."

A challenge simmered below the surface of her silvery gaze, and man, I wanted to win this battle. But it felt like she was baiting me on purpose, and I wasn't stupid. Between her comment earlier about his effect on people and this pointed comment, I was ready to just call her out.

I wasn't sure if she had feelings for him, or if there was history between them, but I found myself wanting to make it clear that he was mine now, which wasn't right. He wasn't mine. I barely knew the guy, and I couldn't stand being around him. Well, that was a lie, but I definitely didn't care about him in a capacity that would lend me the ability to call him mine.

Regardless of my conflicting emotions toward Lincoln, rage and jealousy still bubbled in my veins at the thought of them being together.

I was so damn close to telling her that his erection being pressed against me earlier this morning gave me the wiggle room to use his first name, but at the last moment, I snapped my mouth shut. It wasn't fair of me to throw that in Victoria's face when it would likely get him in a shit ton of trouble. It wasn't like I was given a handbook to read or anything, but professors choking their students and pressing their erections into them seemed like a pretty clear line that shouldn't be crossed.

Besides, if we were going to get in trouble, I needed it to be worth it and not before I'd even had the chance to decide if I wanted to play with him or not.

Shoving my jealousy down, I paced toward the chaise and dropped onto it before painting a smile on my face. “I was told I was here to get a copy of my schedule. Are you able to provide that?”

A soft chuckle came from her as she grabbed a piece of paper off her desk and held it out for me. Reaching forward and snagging it, I glanced down at it as she explained, “Classes for our vampire students are held mostly in the afternoon to accommodate Sanguis operating almost entirely at night. We offer later periods for these students if they need additional time or guidance from their professors or counselors. Which, to be clear, you *do* need.”

I glimpsed over the schedule briefly, to see if I had any immediate questions or if I could get the hell out of here. Happy with the straight forward classes, I nodded to myself. There was relief to be found in the fact that the classes seemed similar to the slayer training I’d gone through growing up, so I shouldn’t feel too far out of my depth.

- Monday, Wednesday, Friday- 2:00 pm **Combat training**
- Monday, Wednesday, Friday- 4:00 pm **Strategy**
- Tuesday, Thursday- 2:00 pm **Praeditus 101**
- Tuesday, Thursday- 4:00 pm **Diplomacy**
- Tuesday, Thursday- 6:00 pm **Mentor training**

- Wednesday, 6:00 pm **Counseling with Victoria**

Rolling my eyes at the last one, I flicked my gaze back up to meet hers. "Got it. Anything else for today, or will we pick back up where we left off on Wednesday?" I asked, pushing to my feet before she could even give me an answer.

This time, a true laugh bubbled from her lips as she placed her pen and paper on her desk. She held her hand out for what seemed like a handshake before admitting, "I think we're going to get along just fine, Alina."

My brows slammed together in confusion, as if she was suddenly referring to a different Alina, or as if she recalled a very different appointment than I did. Shelving my attitude for the time being, I reached out and shook her hand, knowing I needed to at least save face in order to keep my admission to the Academy intact.

Forcing a cheerful tone, I replied, "Oh, swimmingly."

A knock sounded on the other side of the door just as I laid my hand on the handle. Yanking it open, I came face-to-face with a stunning woman who looked to be around my age. Long, black hair flowed to her waist in a pin-straight sheet and warm brown eyes that emanated an inner amber color stared back at me. Her nose wrinkled and upper lip curled in disgust as she took in the sight of me looking her over. "And you are?"

With that tone, you'd think I was the literal dirt on the floor beneath her feet. Like she thought I should be bowing and thanking her for allowing me to breathe the same air as her.

The hair on the back of my neck stood in response to the chilling tone, but before I could offer her a snarky response, Victoria called out from behind me, "Maya, please come in. We don't have long until my next appointment."

My brows furrowed as I shimmied to the side–it kind of felt like Victoria was helping me out and giving me an out. Not only did I not have to give Maya my name, I also got the opportunity to get the hell out of here. For the life of me, I couldn't work out what Victoria's feelings toward me were.

Perhaps she wasn't as bad as I thought, but that didn't mean I was going to be an angel with her. Like Lincoln said, why would I choose the easy way when the hard way was so much more fun?

Also, I wasn't in a rush to let her behind my walls or give her insight into how fucked up and volatile I really was. They would never let me stay here if she saw the truth of what was lurking in the dark shadows of my soul.

Deciding to test her, I shouted, “See ya, Vic,” and held up the peace sign as I pushed past the girl she’d called Maya. A smirk tugged at the corner of my lip as her laughter followed.

It was a subtle dig at how she’d called me out for using Lincoln’s first name. I’d do the same with her, hopefully throwing her off that line of questioning.

My stomach rumbled unexpectedly, and I felt pain in my gums moments before my fangs pressed into my lower lip. Shit, I needed some sustenance. I’d gone too long without feeding, but I hadn’t been in a state to leave my room yesterday to take advantage of the first floor blood bank.

Taking the stairs to the first floor quickly, I heard the buzz of voices floating in my direction. I appeared at the bottom of the stairs, and the noise died to near silence in a heartbeat. Every single person milling around down here was wearing the same uniform that had been in my armoire, just like Maya had been when she appeared in Victoria’s doorway.

Were these my new classmates?

With practiced indifference, I let my eyes sweep over the crowd, quickly determining that not one of them looked welcoming, though they were all strikingly beautiful. Keeping my head high, I walked directly to the front doors, ignoring the whispers of how I was a last minute admission and what I must have done to be granted that.

They could say whatever they wanted about me, creating and circulating rumors that would likely follow me for weeks or months. Truly, it was of no concern to me. Fuck 'em.

As I leaned into the door, pushing the door open, it was tugged open from the other side. I ran face first into an extremely hard chest. "Oh, I'm sorry," I rushed to say, dropping my hands to a rock hard abdomen to steady myself as a large set of hands wrapped around my biceps.

"What do we have here?" a sultry voice rumbled, drawing my gaze up to meet his light green eyes. His dark hair was messy, nearly hanging in his eyes, and I had to fight the desire to reach up and brush it to the side. He had the highest cheekbones I'd ever seen, with a chiseled jaw that wouldn't look out of place on a beautiful marble statue.

Multiple silver chains hung from his neck, easily on display with the two buttons of his dress shirt undone.

"Don't worry, new girl," he purred, bringing his

fingers up beneath my chin, "if you get on your knees for me tonight, I'll forget about this little incident."

Feeling like he'd dumped a vat of scalding poison on me, I pulled away from him. I opened my mouth to snarl a reply, but paused at the sound of Lincoln's voice ringing with authority as he called out from behind him, "Get inside unless you want detention before the year has even begun, Andrei. I don't think your father would like to hear about a misstep this early in the year."

So this devil's name was Andrei. I'd be sure to remember that for when I got to parrot his words back to him in combat lessons.

The tough dude facade fell away the moment Lincoln threatened telling his father about detention, and as soon as he realized I saw his little slip up, he sneered and pushed past me to greet his cronies calling out to him.

It was always the guys with daddy issues that needed the biggest slap of reality. I'd enjoy providing that for him.

8

ALINA

As Lincoln walked up the steps to where I stood in the doorway, I glanced over my shoulder at Andrei. His chest puffed with self-importance as the rest of the people in the room began to crowd around him, making it obvious he was the ringleader of this class. As the crowd pushed in on him, I caught sight of Maya sauntering down the stairs. As soon as her eyes fell on Andrei, her face lit up like she had received her favorite play toy. She strutted toward him, and the crowd parted for her, allowing her to easily plaster herself to his side and bat her eyelashes up at him within seconds. I heard her coo about how much she missed him over summer break, and I barely swallowed the urge to gag dramatically in their direction.

The most intriguing part about the entire exchange is that even though his lips peeled back to smile at her, his eyes were on me the entire time.

So, she was the HBIC of the class, and he was their king. Stereotypical. It was good to get an early read of my classmates, though. It made knowing who to avoid easier, if you were concerned with ruffling the feathers of those with influence. For me, though? I planned on being the HVIC: Head Vampire In Charge–I needed to know who I was taking out.

Sooner or later, I would clash with Maya and Andrei. With my goals, it was an inevitability. I simply needed to lay low until I got a read on how powerful they were and where I stood in the mix with my abilities.

Lincoln's voice pulled me out of my observation and back to him. "You need to feed. Come with me."

Raising a brow at him, I challenged, "I know where the blood is, Lincoln. I don't need you shadowing me everywhere."

His Adam's apple bobbed as his eyes dropped to my throat. "Please call me Professor Aldea."

Interesting. Very interesting.

Dropping my voice to a whisper, I stepped closer to him and peered up at him. "Oh, suddenly there are formalities between us? This morning led me to think differently." Reaching up, I trailed my fingertips along my throat to emphasize my point. I couldn't help but tack on, "I'm so glad you helped me find suitable clothing, too. It would've been terribly awkward if I had shown up here in what you saw me in. Or maybe Andrei and the others would have liked it."

His eyes narrowed to slits as he growled in response to my words. Did he not like the thought of someone else seeing me naked? Surely that couldn't be it. But, in his defense, I'd just experienced an unfounded bout of jealousy with Victoria, so maybe the thought really did bother him.

What the hell was going on between us? It was deliciously intoxicating, whatever it was. I wanted to drown in it, using it to keep my mind occupied in those brief seconds my memories threatened to resurface.

"Keep your voice down," he demanded roughly, his breathing heavy as his eyes flicked between my face and some distance over my shoulder.

I'd bet my life that Andrei was watching us. I swore I could feel his heated gaze on my back. I was probably the only vampire here who wouldn't fall at his feet and thank him for a crumb of his attention. Surely, my defiance would pique his interest and lead him to attempt to figure out how he could break me, inevitably adding me to his group of adoring fans.

I looked forward to seeing his face when he realized he couldn't change me.

Widening my eyes innocently, I asked Lincoln, "You don't want them to see me–" The words died on my lips when he grabbed my arm and yanked me out of the building, pulling me to the middle of the pavilion where it was just the two of us. I smirked in victory as I added, "I wasn't actually going to say anything damning, Lincoln. I'm not an idiot."

But the time for jokes was long gone, it seemed. He towered over me, crowding my space as he glared down at me. "What do you want me to say, Alina? Do you want me to say that I want to rip the eyes out of anyone else who might've walked in and seen you this morning?"

My breath caught in my throat at the intensity with which he made his admission.

He drew a step closer, erasing any distance between us as he lowered his lips to my ear. "Or did you want me to tell you that I went back to my room to stroke my cock to the image of your naked body after dropping you off?"

Oh, fuck, this was getting good.

Desire flooded my body at the image my mind conjured of him, and a small whimper fell from my lips. I wanted to see his head sink back in pleasure as he groaned my name until his cum spilled over his hand.

"If that's what you wanted me to say to you, you're in for a world of heartbreak, *Princess,*" he bit out before pulling away from me, turning on his heel, and heading toward the gate to our sector.

Princess? I was the furthest thing from a Princess, that condescending prick.

There was no way I was imagining the electric chemistry between us. It definitely wasn't one-sided. The heat buried in his words, the way they bit as he spoke through the tension, wasn't an act.

Instead of being offended by his words, I chose violence, calling him out as he put even more distance between us. Despite speaking quietly, I knew he'd be able to hear me. "You're a liar, Lincoln."

Without turning around, his words carried back to me, devastating and gut wrenching as they floated on the wind that blew lightly through my hair. "Maybe I am."

I followed him, letting the argument go for now. As we crossed the threshold to our area, I took my time actually taking in my new surroundings. The paths were paved and lined with dark stone, with the main path leading toward the large black dormitory we were housed in. I found it peculiar that the professors didn't have a separate house, but maybe the academy thought it was necessary for them to keep an eye on us. I wasn't sure how strict the faculty were here, but I was sure I'd find out soon.

What was truly interesting, though, was the difference in climate and temperature as soon as we crossed from the pavilion to our sector. The temperature dropped significantly, a cold breeze brushing over my bare arms as I glanced up at the gloomy clouds I was quickly realizing might very well be a permanent part of the environment. Around us, the trees were barren of leaves, and I found myself wondering if there were typical seasons here or if this was my new norm.

Lincoln veered toward a path to the right that I hadn't yet been down but had noticed when I spotted the second large building in the space the day before. "This is where all of your classes will occur," he explained as we came to a halt at the front. "Except for your session with Victoria each week. That will always be in her office where you just were."

"Ahh, Vic," I breathed out, clasping my hands in front of me. "She's lovely."

I kept my tone light, hoping to gauge his reaction to my snarky comment. If there really was something going on between them, I'd punch him in the mouth for disrespecting her and me like that. If I could, I needed to figure out the truth now.

He offered me a peculiar look, like he found it strange to hear me being nice or something. His eyes narrowed slightly before he nodded his agreement. "She is. Estrid, Victoria, and I have been here since the first year the Academy opened. She does a fantastic job helping our students, so much so that, at times, it almost seems at the expense of her own well-being."

It was clear he held affection for her, but it seemed platonic and based in respect and a high regard for the woman.

I still didn't have a clear answer, though, and I would not leave here without knowing how pissed off I needed to be at him. So I took a chance and asked a pointed question. "Are you two involved? She made a few interesting comments to me that led me to believe there might be something there."

Pure confusion colored his face as he turned to lead us back toward the main building. "With Victoria?" he asked, a dose of horror in his voice. "No. I look at her as I would a sister. I don't have a fam–".

Lincoln's mouth snapped shut, shoulders tensing with his silence. I waited a moment for him to continue, pleasantly surprised that he was opening up to me like this, but instead of continuing, he shut down completely. That same cold exterior from our first meeting in Estrid's office came rushing back, encompassing him completely as he increased his speed.

It was clear that the conversation was over, and I wasn't going to pry. That would be completely unfair of me, seeing as I was in absolutely no rush to share my own history with him either.

Thankfully, it was also clear that there was nothing between him and Vic. And if she also thought of him as family, her questions during our session earlier today made more sense. Considering their relationship, she probably felt protective of him and was able to pick up on little things because she *did* know him so well.

Tension I'd been holding in my chest, unaware of it twisting and knotting there, loosened as I fit the pieces of the puzzle together to get a full picture.

Silently, we entered the building, veering to the right just beyond the front entrance in what I assumed was the direction of the cafeteria. There were tables and chairs scattered throughout the space, and I let my eyes track through the space with quick, concise movements before giving my attention back to the moody man before me. I took the opportunity to change the subject to something lighter, trying to gain valuable information about what I was getting myself into at the academy.

"Can you tell me a bit more about what's expected of us here? Are there any specifics about the way the school operates that you think I should know? Are we given grades or expected to keep a certain GPA to remain? How many students are in each class?" I fired questions at him rapidly, barely pausing long enough to suck in deep breaths of air between each.

Given the massive size of this building, it was definitely large enough to fit more than the amount of vampires I'd seen in the first floor of the academic building. There had to be nearly fifty doors on my floor alone and if that was just for women, then it stood to reason that there had to be nearly a hundred total, not including the floor for the professors.

"Animal or human?" he asked, ignoring my

questions as he gestured for me to take a seat at a table.

It took me a horrifyingly long moment to understand his question, and I stared at him blankly before it snapped into place. “Animal, please. I won’t drink human,” I admitted as I sat in the uncomfortable plastic chair.

With a light roll of his eyes and a shake of his head, he stalked away, walking to one of the large silver fridges that were lined along on the back wall. Grabbing two bags of blood from the first, he tucked them under his arm before crossing all the way to the last fridge on the right and pulling out five bags.

As he crossed the room back to me, he tossed the five bags on the table and said, “Drink them all. I know you didn’t eat anything last night.”

So, he was tracking my meals now. I wasn’t sure whether to be creeped out by his close observance or flattered that he was ensuring I had enough.

I eyed the bags with disgust, not moving an inch to pick them up. Lincoln sighed heavily, pinching the bridge of his nose between his fingers before leaning his forearms on the table. He clasped his hands together, bracing his weight against the cheap plastic as he offered me a placating, albeit patronizing smile "For each bag you drink, I'll answer a question, okay?"

Glaring at him for using my thirst for knowledge in this barter, I couldn't help but get a little snarky as I responded. "As my professor, I'd think you'd have to answer my questions without lording anything over me."

Smirking, he leaned back in his chair. He crossed his arms over his chest, an eyebrow snaking toward his hairline in challenge before he said, "Never the easy path with you, Spitfire."

Spitfire. That's right. He'd called me that this morning before wrapping his hand around my throat. I liked the nickname despite myself.

Begrudgingly, I picked up the first bag, twisting the cap off and closing my eyes before bringing it to my lips. I found that my fangs ached as my stomach screamed for the sustenance. Taking a deep breath, I wrapped my lips around the straw and sucked it all down in one go before tossing it back onto the table and opening my eyes.

His eyes gleamed from where he watched me, the question easy to spot in the hazel depths. "You really hate the one thing that keeps you alive that much?"

Nibbling on my lower lip, I tried to figure out

how to get out of answering that until I could think of a proper excuse. One that *wasn't* the truth. Looking at his two blood bags, I offered him the same trade he'd given me. "I'll answer a question for every bag."

His lips thinned, brow furrowing as he countered, "But I only have two to your five. How is that fair?"

Pursing my lips for a moment, I leaned back and crossed my arms, smirking. "Sucks to suck. I didn't make the rules. You did, remember?"

His signature smirk returned as he drank his first bag. What I wasn't ready for was the way my eyes fixated on his throat bobbing with each swallow. Nothing could have prepared me for the way his pupils dilated in pleasure with each long swallow he took. It disgusted me to drink blood, but something about watching him doing it was way hotter than it should have been.

Clearing my throat, I asked my first question as I twisted in my seat. "How are we graded here? I need to know what to aim for to ensure I get the position I want."

Licking his lip to clear the remaining blood from them, he placed the empty bag down before answering, "There is a running ranking system of the students. It's a point system that you get from each class, all summed up into one total. You don't necessarily have to be the best at every class to get the top spots. You just need to excel at one, and not be poor in the rest."

Easy enough, but I planned on excelling in them all.

"Answer my previous question," he commanded.

"It's not that I hate it," I lied with a grimace. I did hate it. I really fucking hated it. "I worry I won't be able to stop once I start. The hunger feels overwhelming at times."

Doubt flickered in his eyes, but he didn't call me out if he didn't believe the answer.

Grabbing my next bag, I repeated the stomach-turning process before asking, "How many students are in each class? Like, how many am I competing with?"

"Each year we bring in new students for each sector. Classes don't typically compete with each other, at least in other sectors. However, our competitive nature has evolved our system over time, and our students are in one pool, competing for the top spots from year one. Think of it as one big class, with the fourth years getting the opportunity to be chosen for positions with them having the largest number of points accumulated every year."

My brow furrowed as I worked through the answer. Competing with every single student in the sector would put me at a major disadvantage. "Just so I'm clear, it's a running tally system for all four years? That will put me at a severe disadvantage to be chosen this year."

An astounded scoff came from him. "You thought you were going to get chosen this year? I've never seen a first year get enough points to even be considered. Hell, only about half of each new class even comes back for a second year because of how tough the competition is here. Some will drop from your class within the first week–mark my words."

I couldn't tell if his last sentence was more warning or threat, but I couldn't help but retort, "There is *nothing* that could happen to make me walk away from this opportunity."

Either way, at least I had an explanation for the small group of vampires in the academic building and what seemed to be a surplus of rooms here.

A heartbeat later, he tipped his head side to the side, running his eyes up and down the length of my body. My stomach tightened into knots when he stated, "When you said you had nowhere to go if this didn't work out for you, I'm assuming that meant you're no longer welcomed by the slayers."

Swallowing around the lump of emotion clogging my throat, I tried to keep my face neutral as our gazes clashed.

"I've never heard of a slayer being outcast, and I don't think you allowed yourself to be turned into a vampire willingly with your clear disdain..." he trailed off before his eyes flashed with a hint of red. His voice dropped low as he practically growled, "So, were you forcefully turned by a vampire?"

My heart hammered in my chest, thundering like wild horses at the venom in his words. I twisted uncomfortably in my seat, the hard plastic digging into my thighs as I tried desperately to think of a way to lead him in a different direction. He was fitting too many of the puzzle pieces together after such a short time together. Tense silence passed between us for a few moments as the heavy walls around my mind slammed back into place. He stared into my eyes expectantly, and I realized with a start that he wasn't going to move on from this question.

Shoving away from the table, my chair toppled with the force of my movement. I cleared my throat before turning away from him. I turned to go upstairs, done with this little game. I was smart–

surely I'd figure out the rest of the answers to my questions on my own as time went on.

I expected him to chase after me and demand my cooperation, considering the overbearing asshole he'd proven himself to be, but I didn't have it in me to fight back right now.

Grasping the handrail, I took the first step toward my floor as he called out after me, voice calm and collected, "I left your textbooks and an introduction on your desk in your room. I suggest reading those for the answers to the rest of your questions."

He was letting me go, just like that. And he was telling me where I could get the information I wanted. Was he...respecting my boundaries? I appreciated that more than I could even put into words right now. I wanted boundaries in my old life, like desperately wanting to not be matched like livestock to another slayer simply to provide young, but those were boundaries that could never be respected. Being here, with a man who I didn't really understand respecting boundaries I hadn't even vocalized...

Shaking my head at the different sides of Lincoln I was quickly discovering, I zipped up the stairs and toward my room. I slipped into my room, quickly closing my door and leaning against it. I let out a heavy breath of air, relief coursing through my body at the thought of being safe from any further questions from him, at least for now. Just because he let me go this time didn't mean he wouldn't try again in the future. It was evident in the way he looked at me, the way he worded his questions with a quirked brow in my direction, that I was a complex puzzle he wanted to solve.

Spying the books on my black desk, I crossed the room and settled into the chair. Reaching for the top book on the pile, I cracked the spine on 'Dark Imaginarium Academy: Vampires." The small black book creaked in my hands, my fingers tracing the engraved, swirling font on the cover as I settled in, hoping to cram as much as I could into my mind tonight. Anything less than excellence was unacceptable.

I simply would not go into my first day of classes looking like a clueless idiot. I couldn't afford to appear weak or to paint a target on my back. The good news was that it seemed like it didn't necessarily matter if you were here the full four years in order to get a position outside of these four walls. All you had to be was one of the students with the most points in general, and that fact alone was music to my ears.

I would get an appointment with Dracula in one year, even if it killed me. When you had a motivator as big as mine, nothing was unattainable. I'd climb the ranks and claim what was mine at the end: revenge.

9

ALINA

Black, swarming dots littered my vision, dancing around the edge of my peripheral no matter where I averted my gaze. I lifted my head up, neck spasming with cramps from hanging low for so long. I'd spent hours devouring as much as I could of the textbooks Lincoln left for me.

I was pleasantly surprised to find that doing the research didn't feel like a chore. The material I'd read for Praeditus 101 was extremely interesting, and I'd learned more about the different supernatural territories within our plane of existence than I had before. For so long, my sole focus had been on Sanguis, with it being the vampire and slayer territory, that I practically wore blinders about anything outside of it. I'd never known such rich culture existed on this plane, and I found myself wanting to travel to each territory to experience it for myself.

Except for maybe the fae...there was something unnerving to me about them not being able to tell a lie. Everyone lied, even if the lies were small, harmless ones. So in order to circumvent that compulsive trait, the fae had to be sneaky as hell. If I ever bartered with one, I'd probably be somehow tricked into owing them my firstborn child, despite not even wanting children.

However, the most fascinating sector at this academy to me–though their home was outside of our plane–was the demons of Hell. My eyes all but actually bulged out of my head when I read that they would be attending the academy starting this year. I definitely wanted to find a reason to go over to their sector to see what their type of creatures looked like. I mean, seriously...they were from *Hell.* How cool was that?

I'd soaked up the history provided about their territory and how their Queen, Ama, and her eight Kings—yes, eight, the woman had an entire freaking harem—had united two segregated kingdoms, bringing peace to the land. The craziest part was that the actual Devil lost his powers to her when she took over, and they were lovers! It took a big man to relinquish his power and land to the woman he loved, standing by her side and supporting her steadfastly through the transition. I truly hoped I had the opportunity to travel there one day to see how their world worked.

I was surprised that I found the thought of having eight men enticing, though not something I'd ever really considered before. Was polyamory something normal in their culture? Slayers were monogamous, always opting for a traditional one-on-one relationship. And while vampires slept around a lot, I knew finding their mates was really fucking rare. And with how rare it was to find one mate, the probability of having more than one had to be near one in a million.

Stretching my neck from side to side, I groaned in relief as the tense muscles loosened, relieving some of the pain lancing through the area. Glancing at the clock on my nightstand, my mouth dropped open in shock. I'd been reading from the books for the past eight hours. I'd taken one break to go back down to swipe a few bags from the fridge marked animal blood and brought them back to my room, but besides that, my focus hadn't wavered.

At points, laughter had punctuated my focused

silence, reminding me that other students had moved into their dorms as well. At times it would peak, louder and more intense with chatter in between, but it would quickly subside. Thankfully none of the other students came too close to my room, so I'd been able to tune it out quickly once they'd left the hallway for their private spaces.

Walking to the window next to my bed, I peeled back the grey curtain, noting that the sun had set and the only dim light was the circles of orangish light from the lamp posts that lined the walkways of our sector. What was I supposed to do with the rest of my night? I'd learned a great deal from the books, but my brain was brimming with new information, and I couldn't imagine trying to shove more into it. With classes running in the afternoon instead of early morning like I was used to, I'd have to change my sleep schedule to match.

I crossed my arms over my chest as I considered yet another change to my lifestyle, a sullen frown reflecting back at me in the glass. I glanced down as the hairs on my arms stood to attention, aware seconds before I spotted him, that someone's eyes were on me. Standing in the faint glow of artificial light, Lincoln watched, head tipped back, watching me as he gripped a shadowed package in his hands. I couldn't make out much beyond his general features in the darkness, but what stood out to me was the permanent challenge that seemed to radiate from his eyes and body.

I knew he'd been full of shit this morning when he told me that I was mistaken for thinking he'd hate the thought of others seeing me naked, or that he went back to his room to jerk off to thoughts of my body. On our way to the meeting, a spark of insecurity had flared within me when he'd told me I didn't want to know his opinion on the matter of how I looked, but reflecting back on it now, after another handful of heated exchanges...I interpreted those words differently.

He meant I didn't want to know the sinful fucking thoughts he had about me. But the thing was, I absolutely did want to know. I wanted to push him until he admitted them to me, forthright about hating the way he felt. The more I considered it, the more we seemed like two sides of the same coin. He'd made it obvious he hated slayers the same way I hated vampires. Yet we refused to concede to the other when we were around each other. It was a constant battle for the upper hand, and I think we were both a little addicted to the thrill of the chase.

Being attracted to a vampire should have filled

me with disgust and self-loathing. It should have made me feel like the worst kind of traitor to my kind. But for some reason, it offered me a sense of peace. If I ever crossed the line with Lincoln, I knew the result would be a hate-fueled fuck and nothing more. I'd never give him my heart, and I knew he'd never give me his. We'd hate fuck and keep all the messy emotions out of it.

A thrill ran through me at the memory of his fingers closing around my throat, and an emboldened thought took hold. I suddenly knew how I would entertain myself for at least the beginning of my night. Plus there was the added benefit of my little game testing his words from earlier in the day. All silver linings here.

Either he'd walk away immediately, or he'd have a new memory to jerk off to. I was hot for the idea of it being the latter one. Though if I got off in the process, I think I could count it as a little bit of a win-win for me.

Boldly, I pulled my curtains back and stepped fully into the frame of my window. I didn't give myself the opportunity to second-guess my decision. Instead, I grabbed the hem of my shirt and began to lift it over my head slowly.

I dropped the shirt to the floor, a secret smile

stretching over my lips as I stared into the orb of light circling Lincoln below. He crossed his arms over his chest, the unknown object tucked under his arm, and widened his stance in a way that said he wasn't going anywhere. His body language screamed, 'I dare you,' and it made my pussy throb with anticipation for how far I knew I would take this. After all, I was never one to back down from a challenge.

Smiling coyly, I reached back to unclasp my bra, letting the straps fall to my elbows before dropping to the ground completely. Tossing my hair behind my back to ensure he had a full view, I ran my fingers over my breasts, circling my nipples and pinching them lightly.

My clit throbbed in time with the ache pulsating in my core, and I found it surprising how much I enjoyed being on display in such a public way for him. I felt powerful knowing I was in charge of this moment completely. Even more, I fucking loved that another student or professor could walk into the middle of this moment. Lincoln was taking as much of a risk as I was by watching me so openly. Maybe he liked the thought of potentially getting caught as much as I did.

Tightening my grip on my nipples, I tugged

lightly, letting out a soft moan as my pussy clenched. Needing more, I kept my eyes on his as I let my hands fall to the button of my jeans, wriggling my hips and letting them fall to the ground. I stepped out of them, smirking with smug satisfaction when Lincoln's arms fell and he reached toward his crotch, as if he needed to readjust his straining cock.

Yeah, you're definitely a fucking liar, Professor.

Calling him Professor in my mind was such a snarky move, and I couldn't wait to do it to his face in front of my classmates. Every damn time I did, we'd both know exactly how far he'd fallen from his code of honor as a professor at Dark Imaginarium Academy.

I thumbed my nipple, twisting it as my breath puffed from my lips in lazy huffs. With grim satisfaction, I raised two fingers on my free hand to my mouth, sinking them past my parted lips and coating them with spit as I thought of Lincoln standing in the light of that lamppost, shifting from one foot to the other as he watched me, unable to touch himself in any meaningful way with being in public. I pulled my fingers from between my lips, trailing them lightly down my body before dipping them past the stretchy material of my thong. With a low groan, I found my clit, circling the swollen bud as my entire body jolted. I'd take the panties off eventually, but I wanted to drive him a little crazy first.

My eyes zeroed in on him biting his bottom lip as his jaw clenched tightly.

Swirling my finger around my clit faster, I longed to dip my fingers into my core, aching to give myself what I really needed. I was quickly realizing It would be difficult to give myself the performance I deserved in my current position, so I swung my head over my shoulder, eyeing my accommodations as I slowly circled my clit. I caught sight of the edge of my bed just behind me, realizing that if I laid back on it and spread my legs, he'd have a front row seat to the whole damn performance.

Turning around, I sashayed my hips, showcasing my ass as I hooked my fingers under the edge of my thong. Slowly, I bent all the way to the floor as I pushed them to the ground. Reaching up, I ran my finger along the outside of my pussy, teasing both myself and Lincoln, before dipping one finger in and stroking myself a few times.

Touching myself had never left me feeling quite so wound up before. It felt like I was building to a peak faster than ever before. Slipping my finger back out and standing up straight, I glanced over my shoulder to see what he was doing.

His hands were at his side now, one gripping the object and the other clenched tightly. Even with the distance between us, I could make out his blood red eyes staring back at me now. There was an animalistic side to the bloodlust, and I could tell I was riling him closer and closer to that edge, which was exactly what I wanted from him. It was so damn obvious that he wanted me, but I wasn't sure he'd ever cross that boundary unless I pushed him to the very edge of his bloodlust. It would obscure the logical side of his brain that told him he couldn't, and I couldn't help the fantasy that filled my head of the way he'd succumb to his bloodlust, pinning me against the wall and taking my breath away with his hand again while he fucked me into oblivion.

We both wanted it. Hell, maybe we both *needed* it.

Sending a cheeky wink his way, I twirled around, planting my ass on the edge of the bed and lifting my feet to rest against the windowsill. I was beyond the point of reasonable control. Now I *needed* to get off, and everything I did was for me. Lincoln was merely a bystander, a witness to my pleasure but no longer an active participant. I was ready to work myself to my peak and let my body explode in pleasure. I needed it so damn bad.

My back arched as I dipped two fingers inside, curling them up and working them in and out at the perfect pace. Dropping my other hand to my clit, I swirled it in time with my fingers, moaning as I pictured Lincoln watching me from outside. I'd never forget this moment. It felt like I'd fully accepted the side of myself that existed to rebel against all the damn rules I'd grown up with. The desire to free myself from the high standards that were expected of me as the next in line of the Van Helsing house was at the forefront.

Increasing the pace of fingers and pressure on my clit, I felt my pussy clenching as a moan ripped from my throat. I was building toward an echoing crescendo, body vibrating with the need coursing through my entire being. I felt my entire body growing hot, bunching in anticipation of the climax that danced just beyond the reach of my fingers.

Knock. Knock.

With a small yelp at the unexpected knocks on my door, I sat up, wide-eyed as blind panic coursed through my being. Who the hell was at my door? I glanced out the window, trying frantically to locate Lincoln in the darkness. I sucked down a strangled gasp as I saw a figure occupying the same circle of light Lincoln had stood in...But it wasn't Lincoln.

Green eyes and silver chains twinkled under the light, and my stomach plummeted. I'd noticed both of those things this morning after running into him.

Andrei stood beneath the lamppost, and he had his hand down his pants, shamelessly jerking off as he smiled up at me. Confusion and lust coursed through me, at war with the repulsion I should have felt at this turn of events.

Why did Lincoln leave?

Why did I want Andrei to pull his cock out of his pants so I could see exactly what he was working with?

What I did know, however, was that I wasn't even the least bit ashamed over Andrei finding me with my fingers shoved up my pussy.

Recalling his words about getting on my knees for him, I smirked at him as I strutted toward the window. I drug my middle finger up the plane of my stomach and between the valley of my breasts before bringing it to my lips. I stroked my tongue along the finger provocatively before yanking my curtain shut.

He could finish himself off without my help. Maybe he'd run to Maya and demand she satisfy his needs. Even if he did, I knew he'd be thinking about me finger fucking myself the whole time, and that brought me a healthy dose of contentment and superiority.

Tossing my t-shirt and underwear back on, I walked to my door and yanked it open. Finding no one in the hallway, I glanced down to see clothes folded up with a note on top. Dropping down to gather them in my hand, I smiled in glee as I felt the supple leather beneath my fingers.

Closing my door and switching the lock into place, I opened the paper and read the note written in sprawling handwriting. The words flourished in thick, black ink, as if written with an old school feather quill.

"Spitfire, the rules state you must wear the assigned student attire to classes, but I have it on good authority that you might not be a rule follower. Just know there are always consequences for your actions."

Was that a threat or a promise? Both, maybe? Did I really care?

The promise of suffering consequences from him was a damn tempting thought. I wanted him to punish me. I wanted him to try to put me in my place.

Shaking my head at his words, I placed the letter on my desk before unfolding the leathers to see what I was working with. Shorts with attached garters unraveled as I held the clothing up to inspect it. The shorts would look badass attached to some knee-high boots. The other was a simple top with a low cut, scoop front.

It was a sexy look, and I knew immediately I was going to wear it tomorrow. It would lend me the confidence I always felt in my leather outfits, and I desperately needed that energy to help bolster me in my classes.

I'd thought laying low would be the best option until I figured out the other students more, but if I was being honest with myself, I wasn't born to lay low. I was born to stand out. I was often misunderstood, with my hard exterior and soft inside, but I'm hard headed, not hard hearted. I'm a pain in the ass, stubborn as hell, and will challenge anyone, but I'll also love the shit out of you in the same breath because I always care way more than I show.

When I arrived at the academy, I quickly realized I wouldn't be able to pull off the identity of anyone other than Alina Van Helsing, so I wasn't sure why I thought I'd be able to suppress who I was for even an iota of a moment.

I was going to walk into my first combat class tomorrow in this outfit knowing that, just because I was a vampire now and in spite of the terrible things that had happened, I could never lose or forget the slayer I was raised to be.

I could be Alina Van Helsing, a slayer of the most renowned family of vampire hunters in all of Sanguis, a woman who'd been forged through the fires of hell. And I could also be Alina Van Helsing, the new vampire who was about to make my revenge a problem for anyone who got in my fucking way.

Biting my lip as I thought of how thoughtful it was of Lincoln to give this outfit to me, especially after my adamant confession of love of the leathers this morning, I had the urge to kiss him. But that was much too sweet, and the second the image popped into my brain, I cursed under my breath. "Fucking shithead."

I could not allow him to soften my heart. He was still an enemy, even if I found myself wanting to be impaled by his cock at times. He could penetrate me, as long as it wasn't emotional, and this gesture was skirting the edge of what I was comfortable with.

Would it be too crass to tell him to penetrate my pussy and not my heart?

Pinning me against the wall and calling me his filthy slut—that's perfect for what should be happening between us. But to do this? Maybe I needed to remind him of our true dynamic.

I was seriously considering going to his room and reminding him of our relationship dynamic, when the sound of a low groan from the room above mine stopped me in my tracks. Someone was moaning my name, and that someone sounded a whole hell of a lot like Lincoln.

Tilting my head back as I looked up at the ceiling, I tried to hone in on the noise. Straining to make out the low voice, I eventually heard, "Fuck, Alina. Yes."

That was absolutely Lincoln's growly voice, and he was undoubtedly jerking off just as I had imagined him doing after watching me. So he *had* enjoyed my little show after all. So much so he couldn't even stay for the finale. Instead, he dropped off his inappropriate gift before retreating to his room. And that motherfucker actually had the audacity to pretend he wasn't drawn to me when he'd conveniently made sure I was living beneath him.

Desire roared back to life within me, and I settled back into my bed with my legs spread. With even, lazy strokes, I stoked the fire of pleasure burning within me, straining to hear the groans of his pleasure as my name fell from his lips. Lincoln's voice cut out, quieting when my own sounds of pleasure grew louder, announcing my active participation in our fucked up little scene.

Thinking back to being trapped under his body this morning and then to the dirty words he'd whispered in my ear in the center of the pavilion, I cried out, my desire swelling to unimaginable levels. Then, as I heard his groans return, my mind betrayed me. It wasn't thoughts of Lincoln racing through my mind as my orgasm crashed through me.

No, sitting up to see Andrei stroking himself unashamedly was what tipped me over the edge, and I wasn't sure how to feel about that.

IO

ALINA

Checking out my appearance in the mirror, I gave myself a nod of approval, pleased with the woman I saw staring back in the mirror. It was still me, but there was a fire and determination burning in my eyes and filling my body that I'd never felt before.

Today was the day I'd truly begin my mission. Finally, I could lose myself to the grind it would take from me in order to put up enough points to snag a top spot in my sector by the end of this year. Pushing my body past the point of exhaustion, focusing on my target and pushing past my limits was my favorite part of long combat sessions, and I couldn't wait to get started. It was my safe place, and I was glad to have it here, even amidst my enemies.

Empty moments where I was left with nothing to ground me led to dangerous territory where I became lost in my thoughts and memories. If I had to say where I was at in terms of the five stages of grief, I'd say I was stuck somewhere between denial and anger, and that was precisely where I needed to stay. On another, more logical level, I knew I was punishing myself by staying in this mental state. I was finding temporary distractions that reduced my emotional pain in the short-term but provided very little in the way of actual healing.

For now, the distractions were more than welcome. In fact, I couldn't deny that I was looking forward to seeing Lincoln's face when I showed up in the outfit he left for me...as well as seeing Andrei's reaction when he saw I wasn't ashamed that he'd seen me finger-fucking my pussy. Between the two of them, I had a feeling I wouldn't have a dull moment during the duration of my stay at the academy.

Wanting to snag some blood before the cafeteria filled entirely with students, I quickly zipped down and grabbed two bags. Draining them quickly and tossing them in the trash, I realized I hadn't flinched at all drinking them for the first time. I couldn't tell if I was growing numb to my new life, or if I was slowly accepting it. I supposed it didn't really matter which it was as long as I was able to provide my body the sustenance it needed to help me train relentlessly.

Hearing voices from a level above and steadfastly hanging onto the fact that I simply did not want to run into anyone this morning, I scrambled out of the building. I enjoyed the feel of the brisk breeze blowing around me as I walked toward the secondary building in our territory. Knowing I was early for combat class, I hoped I would have the room to myself to do some stretching and warm-ups. I wasn't sure what this first day would bring, but I was going to make sure I did everything in my power to ensure I was prepared for it.

Ascending the stone steps and tugging open the heavy door, I stopped for just a moment to appreciate the ivy vines growing along the old, dark building. It was a beautiful contrast of darkness and light with the old and new coming together. Overall, it was quite charming.

Heading inside, I checked the directions posted on the wall near a flight of metal stairs leading upstairs where classes like Diplomacy and Praeditus

101 were listed. I didn't know much about the academy yet, but I had a pretty good idea that those were the typical show up with a textbook and sit at a desk while someone lectures at you for an hour type of class.

Following the arrows for the first floor, I passed the first door on the left, which was marked *strategy*. The windows were tinted so darkly that I couldn't see inside, so my curiosity would have to be appeased later when it was time for that class. The hallway stretched before me, long and quiet, and I felt like my heartbeat echoed with each step I took forward. I stalled in front of the door at the end of the hall that was marked *combat*.

Reaching out, I gave myself a moment to collect my thoughts as my hand rested on the door handle.

Calm yourself.

Focus.

Trust.

No matter where I started in the rankings of this class, I knew with hard work and perseverance, I'd end up where I wanted. I would simply need to swallow my wounded pride and persevere if my ass was handed to me on the first day. Being a sore loser, sulking about my failures, had always been a downfall of mine in the past. But in this place, with what I needed to accomplish, there was no room for that.

Swallowing my apprehension, I tugged the door open and entered the dark room. Searching for a light switch, I paused as I heard a low grunt from within the space. I wasn't the only one here. Curiosity kept me in my spot, allowing my eyes to adjust to the darkness and search out the identity of the person who beat me here, who was this dedicated. I sucked in a breath as I took in the massive training course laid out in the room beyond the mats I stood on now.

I spotted a dark figure zooming through the course, perfectly executing a forward roll before springing high onto a rope that dangled from the ceiling. Using the momentum of the jump, they catapulted themselves from the rope onto the small platform on the other side of a freefall. The person fell into a crouch, as if they were a damn ninja, and I watched with growing respect as they suddenly shot forward off the platform so quickly I couldn't track their movement. A moment later, I spotted them across a wide chasm that had a safety net dangling between the two sections of the course. This time, they were swinging across a space that you could only get through by using your hands to grip small poles that were spread pretty far apart from what I could tell.

Once through with that, they paused on a small, protruding beam. It appeared that this was the final part of the course, where the person was faced with three constantly revolving sections that flowed together like clockwork. The first was a low beam that would easily take you out at the ankles if you couldn't jump fast enough and land nimbly on the small beam extended across. After that, there were three large dividers that alternated in a pattern of descending, blocking the path. You'd have to time that perfectly if you didn't want it to knock you off course. The last section, though...I didn't quite understand it from my vantage point. Once they began to run through the section, I realized what I was seeing. There were small footholds for the person to use, but each time they stepped down, a swinging bag was triggered to swing from the wall, ready to knock you off course if you didn't get the hell out of there.

A part of me wanted to clap for them when they finished, but perhaps they wouldn't appreciate my intrusion. I opted for quiet admiration instead.

I shouldn't have been surprised when Lincoln's

voice, full of smugness, filled the space. "Think you have what it takes, Spitfire?"

Of course he made the training course look like child's play. He was our professor, after all. He'd probably designed the course himself, running it hundreds of times to make it as difficult as possible for his students.

Feigning disinterest, I popped my hip out and placed my hand on it. "Nah. It only requires agility and course memorization. I'm more impressed by hand-to-hand combat or ability with weapons. Those things show true skill."

I was fairly certain I wouldn't be able to get through that course with the huge chasm to leap across, but he didn't need to know that right now.

Plopping down onto the mats, I began to stretch out my hamstrings first, spreading my legs wide and folding over the middle, reaching as far as I could with my arms. Taking time to stretch over each side, I enjoyed the burn of waking my muscles up. Rolling my hips forward and back, I smirked as the lights flipped on and Lincoln's strangled choke reached my ears.

"That outfit hardly seems decent in that position," he observed.

Just as I glanced over my shoulder, I saw Andrei

swagger through the door with his hands in his front pockets. “Morning, Professor,” he called out as he passed Lincoln, who I, in the light flooding the room, now realized was in shorts only, leaving his well chiseled abdomen, large shoulders, and cut arms on display.

He dripped sweat, and his messy waves of hair were slicked back.

His glorious body didn’t hold for long, though, because their interaction was odd. Had I not been watching, it would have seemed like a polite interaction. A respectful one, even. But the way Lincoln glowered at Andrei as he tugged on a black t-shirt seemed like there was bad blood simmering just below the surface.

Andrei sauntered in my direction, pulling to a stop and standing above me. He stared down at me like he expected me to cower or to hide. Raising a brow at him, I said, “I’d ask if there was something I could help you with, but we both know I helped you more than enough last night.”

His lips parted slightly, shock evident in the way his eyes widened and he spluttered for a moment.

Yeah, motherfucker. You’re welcome for that free show.

He recovered a second later, letting out a low,

sultry laugh that had a shiver running up and down the length of my spine. "You're crazy, new girl."

It didn't feel like an insult but more of an honest observation, so I didn't bother putting any heat in my response. Instead, I opted for the nonchalant truth of the matter. "Sometimes you just need a little thrill to remind yourself that you're alive, ya know?"

Movement behind Andrei drew my eyes away from him, and I cocked an eyebrow at Lincoln lurking behind him, looking like a volcano seconds away from eruption. His face was red, and sweat rolled down his neck, highlighting his clenched jaw and bobbing Adam's apple. The veins in his hands strained as he clenched them into fists at his side, and his forearms bulged. A hint of red crept along the edge of his irises.

Oh damn, I'd accidentally pushed his buttons. What a shame.

Curiosity blossomed in my mind at Lincoln's response, so I decided to have a little fun and poke the bear. I looked back up at Andrei and fluttered my lashes. I sucked my bottom lip into my mouth as I gifted myself a lazy perusal of his perfect form before letting my lip pop back out again. I smiled, voice intentionally husky as I said, "If you get on your knees for me, I'll forget about you being a peeping tom."

Heat flared in his green eyes, and my smile deepened. Hook, Line...meet Sinker. "Can't say I've ever had someone throw my own words back at me and manage to entice me at the same time. Name a time and place, new girl," he tossed out before glancing over his shoulder at the sound of Lincoln's low growl. "Unless you already have plans."

Fuck me.

Was this dude offering to eat my pussy right in front of the very man I had a delicious push and pull with, but who was strictly forbidden?

Students began to file into the room, popping the bubble of sexual tension lingering between the three of us.

A mask slid back onto Lincoln's face as he instructed us to sit and stretch as I was doing already. Andrei took a seat next to me, winking before he leaned over into my space. "Just don't tell anyone about how much I make you scream for me when I feast on you. I don't want a line outside of my door afterwards."

Ahh, there he was. The arrogant prick who was wholly too full of himself. I was starting to think he'd gone soft on me already.

Resuming my stretch, I chuckled, knowing damn well what I was going to say would cut deep for the fragile male ego I suspected him to have. "I'd bet you've never actually made a woman orgasm in your life, Andrei. People are too concerned about inflating your ego to tell you the truth from what I've seen."

Maya's voice cut in at that moment as she plopped down on the other side of him. "Not that it's any of your damn business, but Andrei's very skilled. He wouldn't touch you with a ten foot pole, so keep dreaming."

Rolling my eyes at her intrusion, and the very wrong assumption that he wasn't interested in me, I pushed myself up to begin stretching my back and arms. A shiver raced down my spine, unwarranted, as Lincoln's voice boomed through the expansive room.

"If you children are done with social hour, I'd like to begin class," he snarked, glaring at Andrei and me specifically.

I just couldn't seem to keep my mouth shut. "Apologies, *Sir.*"

His jaw tightened, and the vein in his forehead bulged as I batted my eyes at him.

Andrei chuckled at my side, and it almost felt

like we were comrades-in-arms, on a mission to drive Lincoln up a wall this morning.

"We have twenty-five new students this year, with thirty returning," he announced, finally tearing his eyes away from me and observing the other students gathered in the space. "This year, though, we have one student who is unlike anyone we've ever had in our program before. An exception to the rule, if you will."

All blood drained from my face, stomach churning at the realization of what he was getting ready to do to me. *No. Please don't tell them about me before I've had a chance to observe them openly.*

Unsurprisingly, considering I was the only one not in the fucking academy uniform, all eyes swung toward me. My heart thundered, the beat whooshing in my ear as Lincoln threw me off the fucking proverbial cliff. Coffin shaped nails dug into my thighs, digging in and tethering me in the moment as I silently swore I'd get payback for this. "We have a Van Helsing turned vampire among us. Please welcome Alina as you would any other student."

All I heard was my heart beating, the whooshing blood continuing to pound in my ears. Shaky breaths pushed through my lips as I struggled to fight my pulse back under control. I was going to kill him, it was that simple. His words were filled with malice and disgust, as they had been when we'd first met in Estrid's office.

Suddenly, the outfit and the note made sense. How fucking gullible was I to think it had been a kind gesture. He'd warned me that many students would quit, that there would be consequences for me wearing an outfit like this, staking my identity to it for all to see.

Now I was going to pay that price.

11

ALINA

"A Van Helsing?" Maya hissed as she leapt to her feet, knees bent as if she was ready to attack me now. "Why the fuck should we not kill her where she stands?"

"That is a great question," Lincoln retorted, a sadistic smile stretching over his full, sinister lips.

The fucking psychopath looked like the tension blanketing the room in a choking grip brought him pleasure. I didn't give Maya the time of day, though, maintaining a veneer of calm as I focused on Lincoln. I wouldn't let him shame me into a corner.

"We aren't killing her because Alina thinks she has what it takes to get through one year and claim a top spot. She seems to think she doesn't need three more years here. I challenge you all to have that same attitude; let's see once and for all who really is the strongest amongst you."

A guy from behind me called out, "So it's all of us against her this year?"

Lincoln's voice rumbled with barely restrained amusement. "Exactly. She was raised and trained as a slayer, and you are all the fiercest vampires Sanguis has to offer. It's an age-old battle, and we're here to settle the score, once and for all."

Hatred was palpable in the air around me. It wrapped around me, suffocating in its thickness, and I felt like I was drowning in it. From day one, I'd known this was a possibility, but I wanted the truth to come out when I was ready. That fucker knew exactly what he was doing, and I was a damn idiot for thinking he had even an iota of a shit to give about my well-being by ensuring I was eating and prepared.

Taking a moment to memorialize this moment, I let their disgust sink all the way into my soul. It was what I needed to ground myself, a nasty little reminder that I would never be accepted by them. I would never be one of them. It truly *was* me against the world now.

Fool me once, shame on me. Fool me twice? Never gonna fucking happen.

Tipping my chin up and crossing my arms across my chest, I narrowed my eyes at him, offering my response to everyone in the room. "Bring it."

Begrudging respect flickered in his gaze as I maintained a stone cold countenance, showing Lincoln he couldn't scare me away so easily. He wouldn't make me crumble. I was here to stay, and I was willing to endure whatever he or anyone else threw at me. I was a Van Helsing, dammit—I could take it.

Turning his back on me, he announced, "Pair up. Alina, you and Maya will be partners today."

I couldn't be sure, but I was almost positive a part of him knew that I already disliked the bitch. Maybe *Vic* had given him a head's up from our weird exchange at her office door. There was just something about Maya that grinded my gears from the moment we met, and I would have honestly rather swallowed glass than be forced to be in close proximity to her.

Maya strutted in my direction, standing in front of me with her hand propped on her hip. A perfectly manicured eyebrow came really damn close to meeting her hairline as she spat, "You don't belong here, filth."

It was then I realized that maybe Lincoln had actually done me a favor by pairing me with her.

A cool, calm energy enveloped me as I spread my feet out in a fighting stance, mentally preparing myself for my first real test amongst the vampires. As I sank into the comfort of that familiar calm that sparring gave me, I was reminded of what I would always be: a vampire hunter. I'd prove to her and everyone here that I wouldn't be bullied out of here. And they were damn sure going to understand that they shouldn't underestimate me or let me fall off of their radar with the assumption that I was weak.

Smirking, I ignored Maya's jab, focusing instead on the realization that she was getting more riled with each moment I refused to respond to her.

"The goal of our lesson today is to begin close combat training without weapons. Your objective is to pin your opponent to the ground. The match will end when your opponent taps out. How you get to that point is completely up to you, but remember our one rule: don't kill each other. Otherwise, anything goes."

My mouth widened a fraction in shock at the flippant way he gave us the green light to harm each other in whatever way sufficed, as long as we didn't cross the threshold of killing one another. It took a moment for my brain to catch up, remembering belatedly that we all possessed rapid healing capabilities, so it wasn't quite as dire or fucked up as it sounded in my brain. It was a far cry from the etiquette we were expected to have during our slayer classes growing up, but I suppose it made sense that monsters acted in such a way.

And I suppose that gave me the green light to act the same.

"Go!" he announced.

Maya was so damn predictable it was laughable. She crouched, projecting her next move as she prepared to launch herself straight at me. I easily side-stepped her at the very last moment, allowing myself a moment to enjoy watching her flail before she ate shit. She hit the ground with a thud, and the smug confidence with which she thought she was going to easily take me down with her weight drained from her body.

Shaking my head, I goaded her. "A smart fighter feigns attacks or parries with defensive moves until they can get a read on their opponet's weaknesses. You should allow them to tire themselves out before making your move, exploiting what you gleaned in the beginning of the match."

I knew I sounded condescending as fuck, but I didn't care.

My ears rang as she screeched, propelling herself to her feet and lowering her head like a bull ready to charge me from across the mat. Had she missed the wisdom I just bestowed upon her? I mean seriously, these were supposed to be the fiercest vampires in Sanguis, and she wasn't even remotely at my level. Did her family bribe her admittance to the school? That had to be it.

"Should I get a red flag and wave it in your face?" I joked as I side-stepped her once more, imagining the human tradition of bullfighting. I knew the jibe would go over her head, assuming that she, like most, had minimal knowledge of the human realm, but it was funny to me nonetheless.

As she stepped forward, quickly invading my space, she managed to snag my wrist in a tight grip. Unfortunately for her, her intention with that move was all too easy to read. When grabbing an opponent, the natural tendency was to pull them into you. I succumbed to the pull, allowing my weight to fall into her as she careened her way to the ground. Using her own momentum against her, I straddled her as she fell onto her back, flailing with a look of shock marring her features. I could practically read the confusion over how she'd once again ended up on the floor. Gripping her wrist and sitting up as much as I could, I used my weight to drive force into my hips, effectively trapping her beneath me as she thrashed around.

There was no way she'd be able to buck me off in this position, considering she was a few inches shorter than me and didn't have a lot of toned muscle, at least none that I could easily see. I knew between my weight advantage and gravity's assistance, I had her pinned.

Maya's enraged puffing met my satisfied ears, but I soon realized her protests were the only sounds in the room. You could have heard a pin drop otherwise, and that realization pulled my head up to survey the room. Every single person in the room stood around us in a loose semi-circle, a mixture of emotions on their faces as I scanned the entire crowd. The majority of the vampires held animosity in their gaze, and I could tell a few were tensing, preparing to interfere if needed. There were a few though, including both Andrei and Lincoln, who watched the tussle with barely restrained laughter dancing in their eyes.

Maybe I wasn't the only one who had an issue with Maya.

Fuck, it felt good knowing that the majority of my classmates were getting front row seats to the Alina Van Helsing who harbored a chasm of rage deep within her. As I pinned Maya and surveyed my *peers*, I realized that maybe even I didn't know the full depth of that rage just yet. We'd all find that out together.

"Fuck you!" Maya screamed, and I felt her spittle hitting my cheek as she did.

Dropping my focus back to her, I sneered, "Are you surrendering? If you don't, I'll be forced to make this situation progressively worse until you do."

Her lips peeled back, baring her fangs at me in answer. She gnashed her teeth together like a rabid dog, straining against my hold.

"Okay," I sang, "you asked for it."

Squeezing my hand tighter around her wrist, I slowly increased the pressure until I felt the tell-tale crunch of tendons and bones breaking beneath my fingers. Her screams were music to my ears, and my eyes rolled back in pleasure as I yanked her hand to the side quickly, snapping it completely.

"Are you ready to admit you are inferior to me?" I purred as she moaned in pain beneath me. "Are you ready to admit that *you* are the one who is filth?"

Darkness had descended in my brain, obscuring

logic and rationale as I reveled in her cries of agony and the power that came along with her suffering. I felt like I was on sensory overload, drowning in the pleasure I felt at this moment.

All sound faded from my ears as my eyes zeroed in on the tears streaming from her eyes as I tightened my hand around her currently whole wrist, prepared to give it the same treatment I'd shown the other. My parents would be beside themselves with pride if they were here. I had been forced into a nest of vampires, and rather than backing down from the fuckers when they underestimated me, I showed them the power of Van Helsing instead. These fucking bloodsuckers would regret ever stepping foot into our territory.

Smiling in a way I'm sure looked manic to onlookers, I sighed in bliss as I felt her bones cracking in my grip. The dome of silence in my mind popped unceremoniously as I found myself flying through the air, trying to grasp what the fuck was happening. My body crashed into the wall, and I felt bones fracturing, some surely breaking as the wall cracked with the force of my impact.

My head swam with confusion, a low groan spilling out of me in response to pain pulsating through my body. My ribs screamed in pain as I tried to take in a deep breath.

"Fuck," I groaned, trying to lift my head to see who had done this to me.

Andrei's green eyes appeared in front of me, swimming in and out of focus as I blinked. There were about three Andreis hovering over me, and I couldn't make out which was the real him. I tried to reach out to brush away that damned hair falling into his eyes but was met with air as I missed.

His chuckle wrapped around me, sending tingles of pleasure—which could have actually been pain—through me. Strong fingers stroked my arm before he enclosed my hand in his. "You're not crazy, new girl," he murmured softly, "you're fucking psycho."

Why did that make my toes curl in delight? There was seriously something wrong with me, and I had a pretty good idea that it was likely a concussion.

As quickly as he appeared at my side, he disappeared again. My vision swam, and I blinked rapidly again as Lincoln's handsome face filled my line of sight. I didn't know if I wanted to punch him in the mouth for the position he put me in today by outing me or thank him for giving the opportunity to show the class exactly what they were up against. I also couldn't deny that I loved the chance to take my rage out on a vampire who fucking deserved it. *Filth.* I would've scoffed if everything didn't hurt so damn badly.

I hope she cried like the little bitch she was as her bones cracked.

"Can you stand, Alina?" his deep voice rumbled out.

Black spots littered my vision as I attempted to move my leg just to be met with insurmountable pain lancing through my body with even the slightest moves. "Fuck no," I hissed, "but it was worth it."

The fucker laughed as he brought something to my lips, commanding me to drink. "This will help the healing process. I know you aren't drinking enough for your body to function properly yet."

My fangs broke through my gums instantly, aching to feed and satisfy the constant emptiness I felt inside of me. I didn't realize I was still hungry. I assumed the emptiness was an aftereffect of my vampirism. You know, that sinking feeling in your stomach that comes along with knowing you're a monster.

Ripping the bag from his hands, I drained it quickly. My fingers grazed over his arms, grappling with him as my eyes flew open and I tried to locate another bag of blood. Lincoln handed me another, repeating the process until I lost track of how many bags I downed.

"That's enough, Alina," he said sternly, and I snapped out of the trance I'd found myself in as I regarded him.

I blinked furiously, eyes coming into focus so powerfully that I felt as if I was seeing the world in vivid color for the very first time. I blinked again, gauging whether or not the colors were a fluke. I could smell the sweat coating his skin so distinctly, and the power I felt thrumming through my body was ten times that which I'd felt since transitioning into a vampire.

His eyes swept over me as I breathed out, "Wow."

"As I suspected," he murmured. "You weren't operating at your highest potential because of malnourishment."

Flinching as I saw a fist flying through the air, I dodged to the side as it broke into the wall next to me.

"Improved reflexes," he noted.

"Are you fucking psycho?" I cried out. "You just tried to hit your student."

He rolled his eyes as I pushed back to where I had been sitting before. Quickly, I noted the imprint of his fist, just to the side of where I had been. He'd never intended to make contact with my face to begin with.

"You're the fucking psycho!" Maya yelled before I could call him on being a softy. "You don't belong here."

Lincoln's eyes narrowed, though, like Maya's shout pulled him from his reverie. He removed his hand and balanced on his feet in a crouch in front of me. "You couldn't control yourself once you lost yourself to the fight. You were supposed to stop as soon as your opponent tapped out, Alina, and you didn't. Maya tapped out, but you would have kept going, with glee plain as day on your face, if Jared hadn't stepped in to rip you off of her."

"Who the fuck is Jared?" I hissed, ready to give him a piece of my mind for interrupting that moment for me.

Lincoln's voice went cold as he snapped at me, "You can't stay in my class if you can't follow my rules. Detention. *Now.*"

Shit. It was the first class of my first day, and I was already on probation. I tried to recall the number of detentions a student could have before they were kicked out but couldn't remember what I'd read in the handbook.

"Head to the pavilion. Detention is held on the second floor of the academic building."

Pushing away from the wall, I climbed to my feet, steady enough that the only proof that remained that I'd suffered any damage at all was the Alina-sized imprint on the wall behind me. Lincoln stood to his full height, but I glanced around his sizable bulk, noting the renewed hatred I cemented into my classmates' eyes with that fight.

Instead of feeling bad about what I'd done to Maya, though, I relished it.

Let them hate me. We were enemies, whether I had fangs or not.

12

ALINA

Maybe my walk across campus should have felt like a walk of shame. As I ascended the front steps of the academic building, all I could think was that surely Estrid wouldn't be happy to hear of this slip up when she'd gone out of her way to give me this opportunity. Honestly, the thought of Estrid's kindness was the only reason I felt even a sliver of regret. It was minuscule, and annoying as hell, but it was still there.

I approached the receptionist, asking for directions to detention, and I received an appalled look of horror in return. Must not be normal for a student to get sent here on day one. Hell, it was probably rare for anyone in general to be sent here. Considering how hard it was to get into this school, a normal person would mind their p's and q's.

Stomping up to the second floor, I took a left before pushing open the door to my temporary prison, barring me from attending the remainder of my classes for the day. That fact alone had me considering my actions in a different light. I wasn't upset that I'd put Maya in her place, but I couldn't afford to get behind already. I needed to hit it hard from day one, never letting up, if I expected to claim a spot near Dracula.

As I plopped into a seat, I kicked up my boots onto the desk next to me, letting out a frustrated groan. "Fuck. This day has not gone according to plan."

Thankfully, I was left in the room unsupervised. I took the opportunity to lounge, hands cupped behind my neck as I considered the implications of my actions, which I'm sure was Lincoln's fucking intention. To be fair, a lot of this was his fault for opening his damn mouth and blabbering my heritage to a room full of vampires. I didn't doubt that somewhere along the line someone in my family killed one of the other student's family members. It came with the territory.

Of course that revelation would light the fire of discourse between us. If I looked at it objectively, we hated each other for all the same reasons, but we would never agree on who was right.

Fucking Lincoln stirring the pot.

Dragging my arms down, I shook them out before crossing them over my chest and leaning my head back. I stared at the plain white ceiling, dragging in a deep breath and holding it until it was painful enough to release it. I took another and gathered my remaining rage at Lincoln and Maya and envisioned myself letting it flow out of me alongside the exhale.

There was a line between using your anger to get you what you wanted in life, and letting it consume you beyond reason. I was starting to realize that line was a very fine one, indeed, and that perhaps I was toeing it a little too closely. I'd crossed into letting my anger control me, and that was a dangerous path that could lead to having everything I needed ripped away from me.

Vic would be so proud of me for coming to that conclusion all on my own. Who needed therapy when you could dissociate and evaluate yourself? I'm sure that's what a lot of people who needed therapy said to make themselves feel better, though.

My head craned to the side as I heard the door to the room click open, and a beautiful girl with flowing white-blonde hair poked her head in. Lavender eyes contrasted against her milky skin in an ethereal sort of look. She looked terrified, though, like an abandoned puppy.

Hell, I had to be getting too soft because I actually felt bad for her.

She didn't have attributes that would define which of the sectors she belonged to and was dressed casually, no academy uniform to help pinpoint it. I couldn't help but wonder what kind of creature she was.

At least with her here, I wouldn't be left alone to my own devices.

Raising an arm, I gestured to the empty room and announced, "Welcome to my humble abode. Make yourself at home."

Her eyes darted around the room and back to me as if contemplating whether I was going to kill her or something. Was I that intimidating? No way.

She took a few hesitant steps into the room and asked, "Where's the person who is supposed to watch over us while in the naughty bin?"

My head jerked back at her calling it the naughty

bin. Crossing the space between us, she folded herself gingerly into the seat in front of me, sitting sideways so she could keep an eye on me, I'm sure.

I couldn't help but smirk as I drummed my fingers against the table in thought. She wasn't an asshole, that much was clear. But there was some spunk deep inside of her. "The naughty bin? That's an interesting take on this prison," I mused, wanting to open up a conversation with her further and allow her to hopefully relax.

She would be stiff as a board if she stayed ramrod straight and tense this entire time. My back ached for her at the thought.

Shrugging her shoulders nonchalantly, she explained, "Well, yeah. Detention is for students who break the rules."

It was that simple to her—bless her heart. She was so pure, I felt like I was going to leave a dark spot on her shining soul from just sitting next to her. With a groan, I rolled my stiff neck around until it cracked, and dropped my boots to the ground in order to turn directly toward the innocent girl.

Was she an angel? There was undoubtedly some pull I felt toward her with the pureness radiating from her.

"You sound like you do not belong here..." I trailed off, waiting for her to offer her name.

Sticking her hand out, she offered, "Alexandra."

Pursing my lips, I eyed her offered hand like a snake readying to strike if I reached out. After the way I allowed myself to fall into the allure of darkness and hunger, it felt like a risk to touch anyone right now.

Flashes of Skye ran through my head, and I instantly shut it down, opening my mouth to explain as Alexandra's brow dipped in concern. "I don't have a good grip on my bloodlust. I shouldn't touch anyone with a pulse to be safe."

I swear the girl audibly gulped in fear with that. Fates, how was I going to make her relax? I mean, I understood it. I hated vampires as much as she seemed to, or maybe she didn't hate them... Perhaps it was just fear of the unknown.

Letting out a laugh, I assured her with some bite to my words, "Don't worry, babe, despite being a filthy bloodsucker, I've strictly survived on animal blood since the transition."

Her shoulders sagged in relief as she let out an audible sigh. Wanting to veer away from this topic of conversation, I eyed the bruise starting to appear on her cheek and asked, "Is this a case of 'you should see the other guy,' or did you get bitch slapped and the shit end of the stick with punishment?"

With a roll of her eyes, she blew out a breath and muttered quietly, "I lost control of my powers and could have killed a classmate."

Ahh, it seemed we were two peas in a pod after all. But I seriously wouldn't have pegged her for having that level of power, just from first glance.

Throwing my head back, I let out a true laugh, which felt damn good to do. I hadn't truly laughed in what felt like way too damn long. I loved the feeling of it and found myself shaking until tears brimmed in my eyes. Alexandra regarded me with a quizzical look, and I tried to calm myself so she didn't think I was a loon.

Wiping my eyes of the tears, I tilted my head at the girl I'd absolutely labeled wrong off the bat, offering her an approving smirk. Maybe I wouldn't stain her soul after all.

"Okay, maybe you are meant to be in the naughty bin with me," I joked, feeling myself settle into a comfortability with her I hadn't felt with anyone else besides Estrid so far. "I'm Alina Van Helsing, by the way."

Fuck. Maybe I shouldn't have let that slip so easily. I really needed to consider the weight of that admission until I knew who exactly I was talking to. My knee jerk reaction was that I didn't want this woman to change how she looked at me like my classmates had when they found out.

Nibbling on my lip, I waited for the outburst that was sure to come.

"What the fuck," she screeched before her hands flew to her mouth as she stared at me with shock. Dropping her hands from her mouth, she asked in a hushed voice, "Aren't Van Helsings supposed to kill vampires? Not be one?"

There was something about that statement that brought me back to that night. It was like I suddenly couldn't deny her the ugly fucking truth simmering in the depths of my soul. It felt as if she held the key to my most closely guarded secrets and turned it, disengaging the lock and opening the floodgates.

My jaw clenched as I felt the same rage I felt that night flowing through me like it was happening at this very moment. "Yes, you are correct," I gritted out, settling into the back of my seat.

My fist balled up, hard enough for my nails to cut into the skin of my palm, and I suddenly had the urge to call Devorare to me like I had then, running through the streets as fast as I could for just a chance of saving my family. I hadn't cared if it was me against a horde of the bloodsuckers then, and looking back on it, I'd sacrifice myself all over again if it meant saving just one person.

"But..." I trailed off while closing my eyes and taking a deep, shuddering breath as I tried to calm the bloodlust coursing through me relentlessly in waves. "That was before Dracula orchestrated an ambush on my family, many of them in their sleep, killing every single Van Helsing beside me in one night."

I heard Skye's whimpers of fear like I was holding her in my arms once more, drinking from her neck until she was drained of all life.

I saw my mother's eyes pleading with me to run my sword through her heart.

I felt the pain of Jade's dismissal as she cast me out and refused to end my suffering like it was happening for the very first time.

Fuck, who was this woman and why was she pulling all of this from me? Was she a damn witch? I wanted it to fucking end. This agony tormenting me was insufferable, and I needed her to stop.

Opening my eyes, I hoped I could scare her into getting the fuck out of my head. Smiling sadistically, my hand wrapped around her throat in an instant.

Picking her up by it, I slammed her against the far wall of the classroom.

The fear in her eyes was exactly what I wanted, but for some reason it didn't make me feel any better. If anything, I hated that I put that in her eyes.

Skye's voice rasped in my ear, *"Alina, no."*

My breathing came in rapid, uneven pants that seemed to match Alexandra's.

Feeling the pounding of her jugular vein beneath my hand, I couldn't help but lean in to inhale her scent. She definitely wasn't a supernatural creature I'd encountered so far based on that smell.

I felt the urge to explain myself to her overcome me out of nowhere. "Which is why I'm at this damn academy. To control myself in this transition and become more skilled than any fucking vampire has ever been. I owe Dracula a personal visit to figure out why I was left alive in this fucking misery, and once I get my answer, I'll pierce his black heart with my blade, damning his soul to hell."

Horror washed over me as I realized what I'd admitted to her. I blinked rapidly as I tried to back pedal, but found no way out of it. Swallowing my fear, I dropped my hand from her neck and took a few shaky steps back.

Why now?

Why her?

Why was all of this being pulled out of me despite my unwilling participation in this conversation?

Staring at her in fear of everything she'd pulled out of me, I murmured, "I've never admitted any of that out loud to anyone. It was like the darkest parts of my soul just poured out. How did you pull that out of me?"

Her head reared back slightly as she took in a few loud gasps of air and held her hands up defensively. "Whoa, I'm not to blame for anything other than saying things I should have thought through before speaking out loud. I'll own up to that and only that."

Taking another step back, needing distance from her, I stumbled over the pain of feeling as if my heart had been cut open by my words, bleeding all over this room and painting it black with my sorrow. I fell to my ass, pulling my knees to my chest as my body trembled. I glanced up at her and said, "I'm so sorry, I didn't mean to hurt you."

"I know," she quickly soothed, as she rushed toward me and dropped to her knees in front of me.

Why would she come close to me after what I'd just admitted? What I'd done to her?

She reached out hesitantly to rub my shoulder in what I'm sure she hoped was a comforting manner, but honestly it only served to make me suspicious. Why was she being so kind to me? No one was kind without wanting something in return.

"I'm not afraid of you, okay," she stated with more confidence than I'd seen in her since she walked into this room. "Everything you just said is a lot to have kept inside and to carry alone."

I scanned her face, desperately trying to understand her motives. All I saw was compassion and the desire to help me right now.

She didn't stop rubbing my shoulder, and for some reason, I didn't push her away. Maybe she was a master manipulator, but something in me trusted her, and that was scary as hell. Unexpectedly, it also felt really damn good.

Maybe I didn't have to be alone here.

"I don't have anyone left to trust," I admitted, so softly I didn't think she'd be able to hear it without enhanced hearing, as I rested my chin on my knees.

"I know you don't know me," she stated as she pulled her shoulders back. Determination filled her gaze, and she gave me what I assumed was a no-nonsense look for her. "But you aren't alone anymore, okay? I was alone for my entire life until a few days ago, and I refuse to let you dwell in that darkness alone any longer."

Maybe we were kindred spirits, sharing grief, and I'd sensed that. Perhaps that was why I'd admitted everything to her. There was absolutely no malicious intent coming off of her, and maybe I needed to take a leap of faith and accept someone's kindness.

She wasn't a vampire.

She wasn't my enemy.

Lifting my head off my knees, I pushed a long strand of hair behind my ear, one that had fallen in my face with the position, and offered her a timid smile.

What was I doing? No. I didn't deserve friends. Look what had happened to my lifelong friends. I'd killed one and irrevocably broken the other's heart with the damage I'd wrought.

Alexandra sighed heavily, I'm sure seeing the firm mask I'd put back on, as she pushed to her feet and offered a hand down to me. "I obviously can't force you to accept the olive branch I'm offering—you need to make the decision to not willingly stay in the dark corner of your mind."

Before I could give her an answer, an intercom in the room sounded and announced that we were free to go back to our dorms. That was way quicker than the rest of my school day, but maybe they were operating on the normal day schedule of other sectors.

I could get the hell out of here and retreat to my room in peace.

Alexandra dropped her offered hand to her side and asked, "Are you coming to the party tonight in the demon sector? If so, come find me and I'll introduce you to my friend Alora. We'd be happy to have you."

A party? In the demon sector?

I could satisfy my curiosity of wanting to see what those students looked like and learn more about Hell. Plus, it was in a different sector, and Lincoln had expressly forbade me from going to any sector outside of one belonging to the vampires. I needed to make his babysitting job a little bit harder after the steaming pile of shit he'd dumped me in today. And who was I kidding? A little bit of booze was just what the doctor ordered to numb these emotions until I was able to lock them away again.

Pushing to my feet and brushing my hands off, I settled them on my hips. "I might make an appearance if I can ditch my guard dog of a professor who I'm pretty sure lives to see me miserable."

Surprise shone in her eyes and, as if she thought I was going to change my mind any minute, she linked her arm through mine and dragged me toward the exit. “Let’s blow this naughty bin.”

I needed to be careful of this woman. She made it too easy to think I deserved forgiveness.

13

ANDREI

I sat at a desk that was entirely too small for me, fingers curled so tightly into my palms, I was shocked I wasn't bleeding all over the seat I'd shoved myself into. You'd think with the funding this academy received, they could afford something better than plastic chairs and wooden desks that were sized for adults and not toddlers.

Or perhaps I wanted to crawl out of this chair because of Maya's incessant blabbering about how she wanted to fight Alina again, interspersed with lewd, desperate attempts to try to lure me into her bed tonight. Ever since I'd gotten drunk at the first party last school year and let her give me head, she thought were fucking destined to be or some shit.

When she told the new girl I wouldn't touch her

with a ten foot pole, I'd almost laughed right in her face at how ass backward her statement was. It had been a mistake to let her touch my dick at all, and I would never allow it to happen again. It was like the girl was dicknotized. While I knew damn well that what I was packing and my abilities in the sheets were legendary, Maya had never experienced any level pleasure from me to be this fucking obsessed.

Taking a deep breath, I craned my neck to look over at her plastered against my arm. I hissed, "Shut the fuck up for a minute, will you? Do you love the sound of your own voice that much? Do you get off just from hearing yourself?"

I didn't give a flying fuck if anyone else in this class heard me, including the professor. He wasn't an asshat like Professor Aldea. Besides, everyone else knew and respected how influential my father was. Everyone else *respected* the power I would hold once I succeeded my father.

I'd say everyone could suck my dick, but...Ever since that feisty little thing ran into me yesterday and I saw her masturbating in her window last night, I didn't think my cock was capable of getting hard for anyone else to suck.

Loving the look of shock on Maya's face at my clear disdain for her, I took it a step further and sneered, "I'd love to see you fight her again. It would further serve as proof that you've slept your way to the top of the leaderboard. You may have some prowess and skill, but it certainly isn't in combat."

There were many reasons I had for hating people, but there was nothing I hated more than people who cheated their way to the top. From a young age, my father drilled into my head the importance of knowing your worth and showing it, but not until you could back up the shit you talked.

I saw that same bite in Alina, and to be blunt, it didn't bother me one bit that she had been a slayer. It didn't change the fact that I wanted to watch my cock pound into her tight little pussy. Nothing changed knowing that I would love to feel those claws of hers cut into the flesh of my back as she held onto me for dear life as I gave her the type of punishment the bratty ones earned.

The way she carried herself was unparalleled when compared to other women I'd encountered. Fuck, it made my balls tighten with the desire to blow my load in her.

"Clearly you are all far more interested in what Andrei has to say today than this lesson," Professor Balan surmised, looking over us all with a sour expression on his wrinkled face. "We know you all have a party to get to tonight anyway, so I'm calling class early today. Tomorrow, we will dive into the first assignment of the year, and I won't hesitate to give any of you zeroes if you're too hungover to function."

I wasn't going to question him, loving the idea of getting the hell out of this room. But as we all rushed to leave before he could change his mind, I walked by his desk and heard him muttering, "And maybe I'll get to meet this Van Helsing girl if she can keep her mouth shut tomorrow."

My feet dragged to a stop, and I allowed everyone else to file out of the classroom around me as I considered how exactly I would make Professor Balan understand he was to never speak of Alina like that again.

When the last student turned the corner, I quickly closed the door and appeared in front of his desk as he asked, "What can I do for you, Andrei? You're still on track to graduate in our top spot this year."

Letting out a scoff, I mused as I turned to look him in the eyes, "You truly think that's why I stayed behind? I know I'm graduating in the top spot."

Confusion bunched his overgrown grey eyebrows together. In a split second, my hand wrapped around the back of his neck and pressed his cheek harshly into the wood of his desk. Leaning down to hiss into his ear, I cleared up his confusion. "The only person around here who's permitted to talk about Alina Van Helsing's mouth is me. If I ever hear you speak about her in a crass or unbecoming manner, I will report you to Estrid. If she doesn't take it seriously, I'll be sure to let my father know of your abysmal teaching skills. We can't have the next generation of Sanguis' leadership trained by someone subpar, now can we?"

Sucking in a sharp breath, his voice shook, "Why are you sticking up for a slayer?"

Beads of sweat rolled down his bald head, pooling in the crevices of his neck, and I took a moment to internalize his question. It did not concern in the slightest that anyone could walk in and see this. Professor Balan was a nobody compared to my father. The influence and power were in my court.

I thought back to the way Lincoln had riled up our classmates by revealing her identity and the way she'd lifted her chin in response, as if to say, "Fuck you, bring it on."

I remembered the challenge that danced in her eyes when she caught me jerking off outside and stared up at me this morning like nothing had even happened.

How she had looked ready to pop me in the mouth for the crass manner in which I spoke to her when we ran into each other for the first time.

"Because she is the first person I've seen walk the halls of this school, with the weight of the world resting on her shoulders, and not even flinch in the face of adversity. People like that are rare, Balan. People like that can change life as we know it, and do you know why?" I asked, pressing his face into the desk further.

His voice was unsteady as he stammered, "Wh...Why?"

"Because those are the people who tell their demons to go fuck themselves and persevere. Nothing and no one will get in their way of achieving what they have set their mind to."

With a final shove, I let him go, strolling out of his room to find my classmates gathered at the far end of the hall near the combat room. Focusing on the sounds around me, I tried to pick up on what was happening.

Alina let out a trill laugh and scoffed, "A bitch? That's the best you can do? Why doesn't anyone use the words malicious, vile, or callous? Expand your vocabulary if you want to have an impact, boys."

My cock immediately hardened at the grit in her voice. She'd challenge every single one of us, burning us to ash and leaving a trail of debris floating through the air behind her on the path to destruction. Something was deeply broken within her. I knew that fight in her eyes all too well, and it called to me. When she finally snapped, I wanted to go up in flames with her. It would be glorious to witness.

She brushed past them, keeping her head held high as she sauntered toward me, hips swaying in a tantalizing motion. Her long legs were on display in those damn shorts, and the garters only accentuated the shape and length of them further. As if I could ever get the memory of those beautiful legs spread as her fingers speared her pussy out of my brain anyway, here she was prancing around school in the hottest shorts I'd ever seen.

Widening my stance, I smirked at her as she strutted by and tossed a wink at me over her shoulder, stopping only when I called out, "You going to take me up on my offer from before? Name a time and place."

I was curious if she'd really let me between her

legs. I'd devour her pussy until she thought she couldn't come anymore, and then I would double down and ensure she couldn't leave her room by ensuring her legs quivered until she couldn't stand on them like a newborn deer.

I'd seen the way Lincoln reacted to my presence and my conversation with Alina before the rest of the students joined us. It was too fucking obvious he was into her, but the way he put her at risk, revealing her true identity to the entire class showed how much he truly despised her. I didn't want him anywhere near her. I wanted him to know that he couldn't touch her.

He and I had never seen eye to eye, and I honestly couldn't pinpoint exactly why that was. From the outside looking in, we had a lot in common, with our dads having served on Dracula's board and the pressure that came with that. But for some reason, he seemed to hate me for what I was born into. He hated that I had the world at my fingertips, it seemed.

At least that was my interpretation of the situation.

Turning on her heel to cock her head at me, she asked, "You think you can really prove me wrong about not being able to make a woman come?"

The students, with Maya leading the charge, followed her down the hall, pulling to a stop to gawk at our interaction. I smirked, snapping my teeth at a girl whose eyes were as wide as saucers, enjoying the way she jumped back immediately and Alina's chuckling followed.

Giving Alina my full attention, I closed the distance between us and stared down at her. Tucking a lock of her silver hair behind her ear, I zeroed in on the way her lips parted as she tipped her head back to look up at me.

"Yes, baby girl," I answered, loving the way her cheeks tinted with a blush.

She probably thought I was fucking with her, given the way I spoke to her at first. But that was just the way I kept all the new people far the fuck away from me. They feared my confidence. It was a tremendous weapon when wielded properly.

She pursed her lips, eyes scanning my face before saying, "Meet me at the party tonight in the demon sector. We'll see if you can earn that privilege."

I wanted to drag her against my body and wrap her lean legs around my waist as I pressed her back to the wall. I wanted her to see exactly how fucking skilled I was and how I didn't give a shit who saw. When I set my sights on something, I always got it.

Pulling away from me she walked toward the exit, head held high. "Oh, and Andrei?" she called out softly, knowing damn well I could hear her. "I've decided I'm going to take your spot on the leaderboard, just for fun."

It was adorable that she thought she could surpass me. Even with the inferno swirling within her, pushing her far beyond the limits most people hit, there was no way she could accumulate enough points to do that in one year. I'd been at the top of the game for so long and even I hadn't been able to accomplish what she wanted to do in less than four.

I welcomed her to try, though. It would be fun watching her dominate the rest of these clowns.

My voice dropped low as it rumbled out, thick with desire for her, "I'm not threatened by you, Alina, but I welcome the challenge."

She crossed through the large wooden door but paused before leaving the hall. Turning around to smirk at me, she dead-panned, "You should feel threatened."

And with that ominous warning, she was gone, leaving me harder than I thought my cock capable of being in the middle of the hallway. Students stared at me, eyes wide and stunned at what had just occurred. If I was being honest, I was shocked she didn’t tell me to go fuck myself when I mentioned my earlier offer to get on my knees for her.

She definitely wasn’t predictable, and I couldn’t help but wonder what the night's festivities would bring us.

14

ALINA

My heart raced as I zipped from the school building toward the dorms. I had only meant to try to listen in on the lesson for my strategy class today. After I'd parted ways with Alexandra, I wasn't sure I was actually ready to be alone in my dorm to process what had just passed between us. My heart and emotions felt too raw still. My feet led me to the class I was supposed to be in then, and I had hunkered down outside the door to try to glean any information I could. I suppose it made sense that my default was to go to the place I knew would give me a reprieve from my thoughts. I was the queen of unhealthy coping mechanisms, it seemed.

What I hadn't expected was to hear Andrei not

only knock Maya off her pedestal, but to make it crystal fucking clear how much he wasn't into her. While I wasn't a fan of women being spoken down to, and was an advocate for women supporting women, sometimes there were some that just didn't want that love and support. She was one of them. Instead, she wanted everyone to know their place was beneath her, not at her side as an equal.

A shit-eating grin had crossed my face when he told her he'd love to see her fight me again, if only to prove how she'd slept her way into her spot on the rankings. It made so much sense to me as soon as he said it. She had only rudimentary knowledge and skill when it came to fighting—nowhere near the skill that had been praised by Lincoln when he talked about this fearsome sector.

Coming to a halt in front of the door to the dorm house, I blinked in shock at how quickly I'd gotten here. As much as I despised Lincoln, I had to admit that I thought he was right in saying my abilities had been watered down by not giving my body enough sustenance. A thrill ran through me at the idea of how much stronger I'd be in combat if I continued to take care of myself.

One day I wanted to fight Lincoln tooth and nail,

settling this never ending challenge for dominance that sparked between us.

Strolling into the cafeteria, I snagged a few blood bags as I felt the tell-tale signs of hunger gnawing in my stomach despite having drank Fates know how much blood this morning after being slammed into that wall.

Taking a seat at the table closet to the fridge I pulled from, I wondered who the fuck Jared was. I needed to figure that out and then hand his ass to him in combat class. That guy had splattered me against the wall like a bug, and I wasn't going to soon forget it.

I ticked a mental list in my head, notating who I was going after and in what fucking order. Maya. Jared. Andrei. Lincoln. And then finally, Dracula himself.

There were varying degrees of the severeness and retribution associated with each name, but I would get to each of them. Despite having defeated Maya in hand-to-hand this morning, I knew our fight wasn't over. She just wasn't the type of woman to just roll over and take it. I needed to keep my guard up around her and her cronies because she'd definitely be seeking vengeance. She had a permanent spot on my list for that reason alone.

Jared, I'd take off the list after a fight that ended in me making him sob, begging for forgiveness. I truly didn't think I was asking too much with that one.

Tossing the two empty bags into the trash next to me, I got up and grabbed two more before settling back into my seat. I wasn't sure how much I needed, but I knew I needed to keep a better eye on the bottomless pit that was now my stomach. I wasn't leaving this room until I felt entirely satisfied. Well, at least in terms of hunger.

Shit, my appetite was definitely for more than just blood right now. That brought me to the next person to grace my list: Andrei.

Fuck, I hated that his sexy arrogance was drawing me in more and more. The way he'd flippantly said he didn't feel threatened by me, and even worse, the conviction with which he said it...It turned me right the fuck on. At first I'd thought him as an asshole for the crude remarks he made when we first met. To be fair, he still kind of was an asshole, but I was beginning to wonder about the depth of what lurked beneath the surface with him. The more I thought about it, the more it felt like a front on his behalf.

When he stroked my cheek as he brushed my

hair behind my ear and called me baby girl, my knees had gone a little weak. It wasn't because of the nickname or gesture, but for the depth of emotion I'd seen lurking in his green eyes as he'd done it. The moment took my breath away and was one of the reasons, in combination with the way he'd put Maya in her place, why I'd told him to meet me at the party tonight.

I wasn't sure what the night would bring. Scratch that, I knew it would likely lead to some questionable decisions, but that was exactly what I'd signed up for when I said I'd go and invited Andrei to meet me there.

I could only hope Lincoln would continue shadowing me. The way in which he'd shown his distaste for my conversation with Andrei this morning only made the night's festivities that much more appealing to me. Was I asking for punishment for leaving the dorm? Absolutely. I only hoped my punishment would come in a more enticing form than detention.

With a full stomach, I tossed the final two bags in the trash as the front door opened. Students poured into the building, some headed directly upstairs while others made their way into the cafeteria for a meal. Unfortunately for her, Maya sauntered right up to me as I settled in for the truly enjoyable altercation I'm sure would come from this.

Before, I thought it would be detrimental to be open about who I was. When I put this outfit on, it signaled to Lincoln that I wasn't hiding who I was, and yet I'd still been pissed when he'd outed me in front of the class. But now that the dust had settled, I realized he'd done me a favor. I had no reason to keep my mouth shut if someone provoked me any longer.

Take it or leave it, this was who I was. I had a smart fucking mouth and a face that wouldn't hide how I felt about you.

"Maya," I greeted the she-devil with a serene smile that only deepened the crease between her brows as she scowled, "a pleasure to see you again."

She wasted no time with pleasantries, only stopping when she was a few inches from me. She stooped slightly, jamming her finger into the middle of my chest. "You think you're the new queen of this school just because you snagged Andrei's attention for a few minutes?"

Ahh, so she wasn't even fuming about the ass beating I handed her. It was about Andrei. Funny, her priorities. Once again, she projected her openings, granting me insight into exactly how to push her buttons.

Cocking my head to the side, I scratched my scalp with my nails as I pretended to think hard. "Hmm, I guess if you add up the seconds when we ran into each other Sunday and he asked me to get on my knees for him, and then when he jerked off outside my window last night..." Her sharp intake of breath didn't prevent me from prattling on, "then our conversation before combat class started about how he wants to lick my pussy, and then this afternoon's confirmation reaffirming how he wants to do that still...Yeah, I guess that does only add up to a few minutes."

Bulging eyes and a red complexion stared up at me as I glanced down at her. "Crazy how so much can happen in a few minutes, right?"

My body tingled with pleasure at her anger. I mean, honestly, I wouldn't have bothered with this conversation if she hadn't marched up to me and shoved her finger into my chest. But I couldn't deny how damn great it felt to inhale her rage, letting it fuel and ground me back into the cold, bitchy version of myself I needed to be to get through this year.

A bitchy exchange with Maya? Just what the doctor ordered to feel better, it turns out.

Her body shook with rage and her muscles bunched, projecting her attack *again*, and giving me enough time to crouch down quickly as she jumped up, hands extended to fold around my neck. Shooting forward, I took her out at the ankles, flipping her over my back. She landed on her back with a hard thud, and I quickly jumped on top of her, positioning us into the exact same position from combat class.

My chest shook with laughter as I joked, "You know, based on what I overheard Andrei say and the way you've been in this position with me time and time again, it sure seems like you spend a lot of time on your back. Are you a pillow princess or something?"

"Get off of her!" a prissy voice yelled before a hand clamped around my shoulder, trying to pull me off.

"Let them figure it out Milina," Andrei called out, drawing my attention to where he casually leaned against the wall to our left, observing the exchange with a feral grin.

I swear this was like a wet dream of his,

watching me destroy Maya without even truly trying.

"But..."

I glanced over my shoulder to find an unfamiliar girl flapping her mouth open and closed. Her hair was a mixture of blonde and caramel highlights twining together, contrasting against her tanned skin. Her brows knitted together as she glanced between Andrei and where Maya was pinned beneath me, as if trying to decide which of her rulers to listen to.

She made the wrong choice when her hand tightened once more on my shoulder as she adamantly said, "Fuck off, Andrei. Maya is my friend."

Maya huffed with indignance beneath me as she squirmed, once again finding she wasn't getting out of this position.

"Shut up, Milina," I groaned, annoyed with her intrusion. "Your name is like the knock off of mine. You ever heard of Target and Walmart in the human realm? I'm Target, and you are Walmart. You might even be the Dollar General, jury's still out."

Man, I really wished she hadn't shown confusion at the end of that. It was such an incredible burn to anyone who understood the comparison. My humor was wasted in this realm, it seemed. Pity. If I thought there was a life for me on the other side of my revenge, I'd happily go live with the humans and make my daily routine visiting Target, Hobby Lobby, Starbucks, and Chick-fil-a. Maybe the basic bitch life was for me. Jade, Skye, and I had definitely stayed in their realm for too long when we were on missions there, but it was hard to not satisfy our curiosity while we could.

"What is going on here?"

Lincoln's scolding voice rang out, making me sigh heavily, knowing my fun was going to be over now that daddy was here. He really did carry around big dad energy, reprimanding us and overall just not letting us have fun.

Jumping up and knocking Milina out of my way, I put my hands behind my head and feigned innocence. "Oh, just having a snack before bed."

Bed? Really, that's the best you could come up with, brain? It's like 5pm.

His lips thinned as his eyes narrowed on us all, ending with Maya who was pushing herself off the ground. "Ms. Federman, are you okay?"

The scalding look she shot my way was indication enough that she was about to rat me out like a little bitch. “Alina attacked me! It was completely unwarranted.”

Lincoln’s chest rose as he took a deep breath and pinched the bridge of his nose, clearly annoyed that he had to deal with this right now. That made two of us. “Is that true, Ms. Van Helsing?”

“Sir,” I started, making his eyes snap open and dilate as I continued, “I would never do anything that would result in you punishing me. I learned my lesson earlier.”

We both knew that was a load of bullshit, and I was delighted to see that he couldn’t hide the slight smirk tugging up the left side of his mouth. Dark stubble shadowed his chin and cheeks, and I found myself unabashedly wondering what it would feel like between my thighs. I wasn’t sure if the rough texture would feel amazing or if it would tickle, but color me curious either way.

Andrei coughed, “Bullshit,” from behind me, poorly covering the word as he cleared his throat. Without turning around, I flicked him off behind my back.

We all knew I was full of shit, but it was up to Lincoln to decide whether he wanted to push the issue.

To my utter shock, he ran his hand through his

curls, sighing with resignation before saying, “Alright, clear out and go back to your dorms. Don’t be complete idiots at the party tonight.”

Some of the rebellion sparking within me fizzled out at the thought of him already knowing about the party we were planning to attend. I’d have to *really* rile him up with Andrei if I was going to get anywhere close to even with him for how dirty he did me earlier. It was like a two-for-one special. I’d ease some of this damn sexual tension with Andrei and piss of Lincoln in the process.

If he couldn’t tell from last night, I had no problem putting on a show for him. And this act? It would be my best one yet.

15

ALINA

Sometimes moments seemed so trivial until, suddenly, they transported you back to another time in your life. When things were great, you took too much for granted. And then, out of nowhere, you felt so much anger with yourself for not appreciating what you had back then, wondering the entire time why the fuck you weren't grateful when you should have been. Why wasn't it enough?

As I stood in my room, needing to get ready for the party, I fell into the same pattern I would have if I had been home with Jade and Skye in the manor. First, you picked an outfit, then you matched your makeup to it before deciding what hairstyle fit the overall vibe.

I stood, staring into my armoire and seeing nothing but academy clothes and the basics. After settling for keeping my current outfit on, I headed to the small ensuite bathroom, only to realize I had no makeup here and no tools to fix my hair.

The worst part, though? The fact that I didn't have my two best friends at my side, giggling and singing along to the music coming from the speaker that would have been blaring. Getting ready was often the best time of the night. There was always an air of excitement, a just-there presence of the what-ifs of what the night would bring us.

Placing my hands on the white laminate countertop, I stared into the mirror and pleaded with myself to not dwell in this moment. To not let it crash through me like waves breaking over and over again, unrelenting and threatening to drag me under.

My two options were to either go to the party, maybe losing myself to some inhibitions, or stay in this room alone and remember just how fucked up my life had become.

Maybe resorting to losing myself in hatred and sexual need in an effort to numb out everything that threatened to claw its way out of me every day wasn't the healthiest way to cope. But today, specifically my time with Alexandra, had brought everything back from that awful night in quick succession, not giving me a moment to truly grasp what was happening. I didn't get the option of preventing it from ripping out of me, and I was forced to go along with it, like a passenger on a runaway train.

If that hadn't happened, I think I might have been able to spend the night in my room and bury my head in the books on my desk again. But the idea of being stuck in these four walls for another night made my skin crawl. The boundaries were suffocating, and it felt like the walls were closing in on me, shrinking in with each passing moment.

Turning the sink on, I splashed cold water over my face, trying to shock myself out of this pity party before toweling the water away. Using the comb provided by the school, I was able to at least brush out all the tangles in my hair and tame it into a somewhat presentable state. I was lucky that my hair was naturally pin-straight and low maintenance.

While I wished I had makeup to give me an extra confidence boost tonight, it wasn't the end of the world. I had always thought of it as war paint, though. There was just something about finishing off your makeup and standing back to take in a bolder, more assured version of yourself staring back at you. It always made me feel invincible.

Crossing the room to glance outside, I noted the setting sun and figured it couldn't hurt to grab a few bags of blood to drain before setting out for the party. I was equal parts nervous and excited to see Alexandra again and to meet her friend Alora.

It would be nice to have people I could consider acquaintances at the academy. I knew I wouldn't allow myself to grow close enough to be considered friends, per se, but it would be comforting to have people to escape to if I needed a break from my own sector.

Making quick work of fueling up on blood, I glanced around curiously as I realized no one was around. Maybe the vampires were those stereotypical types who thought it was cool to show up late for everything. Or maybe they were pre-gaming. That would be fun, you know, if I was invited and didn't hate everyone.

As soon as I stepped outside of our building, Lincoln was there, wrapping his fingers around my throat, pulling a soft moan from me as he gave me exactly what I wanted from him. But as he propelled me toward the side of the building, ready to pin me against it, I tracked his movements better and flipped us at the last minute, slamming his back against the wall.

A low chuckle vibrated his chest as he shook his head at me. Mirth colored his eyes as he said, "I was going to ask if you were planning to be a good girl tonight, or if you were going to make my life a living hell. I guess I have a clear answer to that question."

His eyes drank in the length of my body as I purred, "It's only fair that if you make my life hell, I get to return the favor. Sounds fair, right, *Sir*?"

Was it even possible to hit him back in the same way he'd done to me, though? What could I possibly do to make everyone around us hate him, setting a target on his back and leaving him feeling like he was walking on the jagged pieces of broken glass in the very place he was expected to live for the next *several* years. There was no escape for me, and he'd ensured that.

My tactics to rile him up were childish at best. This was a case of making him want me and then not letting him have me. It was such petty shit at the end of the day, but it's all I had against him...and how pathetic was that?

A rumble spread through his chest, his voice dropping low, "I like when you call me that, Spitfire.

It shows me that you understand I'm the one in charge here."

I should have let myself fall into the natural banter we had. It should have been the same old, same old between us. But this time, it felt like nails on a chalkboard, and my skin crawled in response to his words.

With a roll of my eyes and a huff of indignation, I pushed away from him and sauntered towards the exit of our sector, ready to grab a drink and lose myself in music and dancing for a bit. I couldn't pinpoint why exactly I felt an overwhelming annoyance with him. This is what we did, our never ending push and pull. So why did I feel like he'd let me down, and why was it just now hitting me?

Fucking Alexandra and whatever she did to make me have softer emotions was clearly bubbling over into other aspects of my life now.

"That's it?" he called at my retreating back, clearly as confused as I was at the lack of response.

Something broke in me at his question, and I whirled around, letting my anger and frustration flow out, barely breathing between my choked words. "What?" I spat at him, pacing like an angry cat in front of its prey. "You don't like that I can't just reconcile the fact that I thought you actually gave a shit about my wellbeing in your own weird, convoluted way, to see today that you actually enjoyed feeding the hatred my classmates felt toward me, turning them on me and making my life a thousand times harder than it already is?"

His expression fell before shuttering, which spurred me on further. "Am I supposed to thank you for that?" I huffed, throwing my hands in the air. "I keep making excuses for why I should give this toxic thing between us any of my time. The truth is, if I wasn't fucking broken inside, I would never have entertained you after you made your disgust for who I was was blatantly obvious in Estrid's office."

My voice tapered toward the end of that rant, diminishing until it was barely a whisper as I acknowledged the truth of what this thing was between us. Surely the fact that he challenged me and didn't roll over for me in an instant, wasn't enough of a reason to excuse everything else. Was I truly doing myself any favors by using this outlet as a crutch for my emotions?

A dark laugh burst from him, making the skin on the back of my neck prick with unease as he took a few long strides in my direction, easily eating up the distance between us in seconds. "You think I want to feel drawn to you, Princess? I fucking hate your kind," he hissed out, and my eyes narrowed at his tone.

"Yes, I want you the fuck out of the academy," he admitted, bringing his fingers up to grip my chin tightly, tipping my head back and forcing my gaze up to his. My lips parted as I drew a shuddering breath, heart pounding in recognition of the inferno of hatred and lust swirling in tandem in his eyes. "I want to get you away from me because you're in my head every waking and sleeping moment of my fucking day. I want you out of the academy so Andrei can't run his eyes over your body, imagining everything he wants to do to you."

His words faltered, and for a quiet moment, we just stood there, breathing heavily and staring into each other's eyes.

He spoke then, voice cracking and clogging with the depth of his emotion, and my heart stalled in my chest. "I want you out of the academy so that you won't get hurt."

I spluttered at his admission, heart reigniting in my chest and exploding into double time as a tired sort of anger burned through my gut. "You don't want me to get hurt? So what, you tell everyone exactly who I am so they'll ask me over to braid my fucking hair and paint my nails? The entire sector turned their wrath on me, so yeah, obviously your reasoning makes perfect fucking sense, Lincoln."

His lips thinned as he growled and moved his hand from my chin to the nape of my neck before slipping his fingers into my hair and yanking my head back. I let out a hiss of pain but secretly loved the feeling of it.

"I knew you'd choose the outfit that made you feel like a slayer, Alina. I knew you'd refuse to hide who you were to conform to what you needed to be to survive here. It's why I want to pin you on your back and sink my cock into you, Princess. You're wild and untamed. You are unashamedly *you.* You would never be able to hide who you are, and it was best for it to come out on our terms."

That was exactly what I had said to Estrid, but I had never once thought it was what Lincoln was thinking when he'd outed me.

My chest heaved, a confusing mixture of my anger and desire pushing my chest down and making it difficult to draw the next breath. Anger still simmered in my blood over his actions, but fuck me if his words didn't make my pussy throb with desire. I wasn't sure who made the first move, but a second later, our mouths clashed in a flurry of hatred and need. His tongue speared into my mouth, dominating me as I moaned, nipping at his lip as he tried to pull away.

Another growl fell from his lips, and suddenly both of his hands were tangled in my hair as we devoured each other. Our teeth clashed and my lip bled when his fang nicked my lip, splitting it open. Blood poured into my mouth and down my chin, and though I tried to back away, he doubled down, lapping at my blood and groaning in ecstasy.

I felt the bloodhaze come over me, heightening my emotions and urging me to give into my more animalistic nature. With a growl, I nipped him back, feeding the urge to mark him and drink from him the same way he'd done to me.

White hot desire flooded me, and I swore our souls hovered somewhere above our bodies for an intense moment. Energy surged through me, and it felt like we'd suddenly become one, twining together until there was no untangling who we were without each other anymore.

Heat seared through the back of my neck, bringing me back to my conscious state and forcing me away from Lincoln. Stomach clenching, I took a step back as I tried to figure out what was wrong with me. My hand flew to the back of my neck, and I realized a half second later that he mirrored my movements.

What is wrong with me?

Why is he doing the exact same thing as me?

Out of nowhere, I heard his voice in my mind, and I wouldn't have believed it if I couldn't see that his mouth wasn't moving at the exact moment I heard him.

No. No, this cannot be happening.

"What's going on?" I demanded. "Why can I hear your thoughts?"

His eyes widened in horror as he took two steps back, seemingly fearful of me for the first time ever. I felt his emotions pouring through me in a tumultuous wave. Fury. Disbelief. Joy. Trepidation.

The wave of emotion was so overwhelming it brought me to my knees. Chest heaving, I stared up at him, fighting to figure out which of the emotions and scrambled thoughts slamming through me at the moment were my own.

Lincoln turned, racing towards the dorms as peaceful silence washed through me.

He'd left me.

Heat flushed my face as tears pricked my eyes. I'd let him in for the briefest moment. I'd crossed the line I swore I wouldn't with Lincoln, and he'd left me here alone, scrambling to understand what the fuck had just happened.

It was clear he wasn't capable of processing his own emotions, so why the fuck did I think he'd let me in? Wiping at my tears angrily, I pulled the mask of cold nothingness back over my face and yanked up the wall at the center of my mind.

Pushing to my feet, I raced back into the cafeteria, desperate for a napkin to wipe away the evidence of our mingled blood before leaving for the party. Now more than ever, I needed a stiff drink and music to help me forget about that infuriating vampire.

He didn't get to just pick and choose when to be open with me. If he wanted to walk away from me when I needed him most, I'd never give him the chance again.

16

ALINA

Walking through the gate between our sector and the pavilion, I stopped in my tracks at the sight of the swarms of different creatures heading toward one specific gate near to the academic building. That had to be the demon sector.

Two huge, grey wolves were play-fighting, it seemed, in the middle of the courtyard. They pounced on each other, rolling around as they yipped and barked back and forth, occasionally nipping at one another's back legs. Ethereal looking humans with pointed ears and various colored, semi-translucent wings flew through the air with wooden barrels dangling between them.

Behind me, a vampire came through the gate,

bumping into me before huffing, "Get the fuck out of the way."

Taking a deep breath, I forced the initial need to argue with them down. Speeding over to the demon gate, I passed through it, immediately feeling the heat of their climate licking at my skin. I was so damn thankful I hadn't switched into jeans now. As sweat pooled at the small of my back, I couldn't help but wonder if they were trying to simulate the actual environment of hell, because *damn.* I wasn't sure how long I'd last in this heat.

A beautiful forest lay before me, fairy lights twined around trunks and through branches, lighting up the space just enough, while setting a beautiful atmosphere. The pulsing bass of music drew me towards the throng of students conversing, and I found myself wondering why it was forbidden to fraternize. Everyone seemed to be mingling perfectly.

Two burly dudes took the barrels from the creatures I assumed were fae, cracking open the lids and calling out, "Now the party is really starting! Fae wine is never a miss."

I wasn't a big fan of wine, much preferring the burn of bourbon or whiskey, so I passed by them to where a line formed a little further down the dirt path, starting at a long table that seemed overflowing with liquor bottles.. As the line trudged on, I kept an eye peeled for Alexandra or Andrei. They were the only faces I'd welcome in my currently soured mood.

The final rays of sun had disappeared behind the skyline by the time I got to the front of the line and ordered a glass of whiskey with an ice cube to chill it slightly. "You sure you don't want a mixer?" the pale girl bartending asked with a pointed look. She had the most stunning icy, light blue eyes I'd seen, and I'd been distracted, trying to work out what she was with the tendrils of shadows wrapping around her hands as she moved.

Grimacing with the embarrassment of being caught staring, I confirmed, "Yeah, it's been one of those days."

With a shrug, she filled the cup to the top and responded, "Cheers to that. Hope it gets better for you."

"Thanks," I murmured and moved out of the line, taking two large swigs of the dark liquid and loving the instant burn in my throat and chest.

With a slight shiver at the shock to the system it gave me, I moved toward the music, drawn to it like a magnet. I slipped onto the dance floor someone had created, doing my best to not spill any of my drink as I squeezed through the mass of grinding bodies. Finding a pocket of emptiness, I let my head tilt back as the electronic, thumping bass vibrated through my feet, starting in my ears and feet and meeting somewhere in the middle until my entire body buzzed. I swore there was nothing that helped me let everything in my mind go as quickly as losing myself to music. Swaying my hips in time with the beat, I stayed there for what could have been minutes or hours. All I knew was that by the time I lifted my glass to my lips and finally found it empty, I was a sweaty mess. My hair stuck to the back of my neck, and I had to wipe my brow from the sweat trickling down it.

At this point, I was finally starting to feel the numbness of the alcohol settling in, and I knew it would help me release my inhibitions and level out into a more pleasant mood, despite what had happened with Lincoln. In my head, everything on my mental plate that should be left for another time didn't exist in this moment of my life. It could all wait.

Excusing myself as I pushed to the edge of the floor, I realized no one had once tried to cop a feel or grind against me while I danced. That was rare, and

I was so damn appreciative that no one had popped that bubble of happiness for me.

The line for drinks was long as hell now, but I definitely wanted one more glass for the night, so I settled in for the long haul at the end. The two guys in front of me were chattering away about their first day of classes, and I picked up on them talking about how Alexandra had whooped this hellhound's ass. I felt a swell of pride in my chest for her. Their conversation shifted to how attractive Alora was, and my ears piqued at the mention of her friend.

“Man, she’s so fucking hot. But I wouldn’t risk getting my dick chopped off by her eight dads.”

My brow rose. Eight dads? Why did that sound familiar?

“You’re afraid of her dads?” the one on the left scoffed. “Nah, dude, her mom is the fucking Queen of Hell. That’s who you should fear.”

My eyes practically bugged out of my head as all the pieces fell together. I’d read about Queen Ama and her eight mates. Alora was their daughter? Holy shit.

Whipping my head on either side of the line, I scoured the bodies milling around for any sign of Alexandra, wanting more than ever to meet Alora. I needed to pick her brain so badly.

Unfortunately, I still didn't find her by the time I got my second drink, accompanied by a smirk from the bartender. I couldn't deny that I felt a little crestfallen at that. Deciding to stand away from the crowd for a while, I walked through the forest until I found a clear spot to look up into the sky.

Standing in a near-ethereal moment of quiet, I sipped on my drink until shouts and howls sounded from somewhere near enough to draw my attention from the dark, sparkling night sky and my thoughts. Figuring I could use some excitement, I made my way toward the treeline near the dance floor, which is where the commotion seemed to be coming from.

A petite blonde stood exactly where I had planned on making myself comfortable, but the alcohol blazing through my veins made me a little more tolerant of being around people, so I didn't change my course.

I heard the man who deposited her there say, "Stay here with the girls; I have to break this up. Stupid fucking wolves."

Standing just a few feet away from her, I acknowledged his knight in shining armor persona. "That's nice of him."

If you wanted to be coddled and told what to do, that is. But hey, if she was into that, I was happy for her. Me? I had the itch to insert myself into the fight, but it was becoming very clear I didn't have the best judgment, so maybe it was better to stand back and observe.

Her hair fanned out around her as she startled and looked back at me before she asked, "What?

"Your guy, going to break that up," I explained, lifting my drink and gesturing toward where he'd gone. "I was sort of hoping it would get more violent before someone stepped in."

Moving my glass to my lips, I let the liquor burn a trail of fire down my throat and into my chest.

The woman seemed genuinely curious about me, or at least of what I was saying, as she walked closer to me and asked, "Why?"

Maybe we'd graduate to more than one word questions next.

"It's entertaining," I offered and flashed her a smile, no doubt showing my fangs off because damn was it hard to keep those fuckers contained when there was alcohol in me. They had a mind of their own. I wasn't even hungry, but they refused to be retracted.

"You're a vampire," she breathed out in awe, but there was the air of a question mark at the end of that, like she needed confirmation.

There was no denying that, much to my disgust. Letting out a dry laugh, I conceded, "Yeah... I guess I am."

She frowned, tilting her head to the side as she asked. "You guess?"

Ahh, there we were. Onto two word questions now.

"Doesn't matter," I answered in a dismissive manner, flicking my long hair over my shoulder as the heat of this sector began to make my skin prick with sweat again, despite getting a slight breeze being away from the mass of bodies. The girl looked a little off put with that answer, so I raised a brow and offered, "Not quite used to admitting that yet."

She lit up at that, though I wasn't sure why.

"I'm Bexley," she said, offering a small smile. "But you can call me Bex."

Running my eyes over her, I lifted my nose up to catch the scent on the wind, trying to figure out what she was. There was definitely power flowing through her, but also a very woodsy scent accompanied with it and was that...fire? Some type of burnt scent.

I'd bet she was a shifter.

Offering her a smile of my own, to try to not be

such an off-putting asshole, I offered, "Alina. You're a shifter?"

"Yes..." she answered after a moment of hesitation, before her brows knitted together and she tacked on, "Sort of?"

"Sort of?" I mused before taking a sip of my drink again and scanning the crowd in front of us. None of the fun was making its way any closer to us. Shame.

"I have never shifted," Bex admitted softly, like she was ashamed of that, pulling my attention back to her.

So she was a shifter who had never shifted, and I was a vampire who hated vampires. What a conundrum we were in, in this place we were temporarily calling home.

Offering a hum of amusement, I observed, "Well, it seems that neither of us fit in with our people."

It was nice, knowing that I wasn't the only one here struggling with being the outsider.

"Yeah, you're right."

The big man from before broke from the crowd and made his way toward us, his eyes only focused on the tiny woman in front of me. I knew she wasn't going to be here much longer, so I might as well get the goodbyes out of the way now.

"It was nice to meet you, Bex. I am going to head out. It seems you may be as well. I hope we cross paths again soon. If you ever find yourself in my sector, just ask for the crazy bitch. They'll point you in my direction."

I truly meant it. Being around her was easy, and it seemed like we easily understood one another with little time or words. Sometimes, those were the best types of relationships. The ones where you didn't need to fill the void with useless chatter to feel comfortable. Where you could just stand in someone's presence and feel at ease.

"And if you come to the shifter sector, just ask for the shifter that doesn't shift and lives with dragons," she offered, giving me a sweet smile as the guy called out her name.

Dragons definitely explained why she smelt somewhat charred to me. They must be around her a lot to give off such a strong scent without her being next to them now. Maybe I'd take her up on that offer and visit one day. I wouldn't mind seeing a dragon in the flesh. Maybe if I was nice they would give me a ride...or maybe that was rude to think. Who fucking knows.

Zipping away, I realized I wasn't going to run into Alexandra at this point. I supposed I could search for Andrei now that I was mentally lubricated.

Walking around, I eventually spotted a crowd of vampires standing around a table with a bunch of plastic cups on it. My eyes tracked white balls being tossed through the air before landing in a cup on the other side. Cheers sounded as a few fists pumped toward the starry night sky, and I finally spotted Andrei's, standing alone on the side that still had a bunch of cups on it. Glancing at the other side, I spotted his opponent, head hung low in defeat as he removed the ball from the final cup, drinking whatever contents filled it.

Sidling up to Andrei's side, I tossed out, "Nice job," to get his attention.

Whirling around, he placed his hands against the table and leaned back, his stance cocky as he asked, "Do I get a kiss for my prize, new girl?"

Pondering it for a moment, Lincoln's face swam to the front of my mind for a millisecond, and I took a step forward to give Andrei exactly what he asked for. I paused when I realized I couldn't get my damn fangs to retract. I didn't want to nick him, and so my mind swam through all of the reasonable and unreasonable things I could do to make the fuckers go away. Finally, I landed on the most logical thought my semi-hazy brain could come up with, maybe they'd go away if I relaxed more.

"Why don't we go somewhere quieter?" I offered coyly, wanting the opportunity to actually talk to him without the sneers of our peers surrounding us from all directions.

Undoubtedly, I was physically attracted to Andrei. I realized that there was more to him than I initially realized. He was more than a pretty face, and I was beginning to see that with each interaction.

"Lead the way, baby girl," he said, pushing to his feet and crossing the distance between us. He threw his arm around my shoulder, tucking me into his side as we walked away from the gathered vampires.

My cheeks flushed at the intimacy of the touch. It left no room for anyone else to question whether he was claiming me, but not in a suffocating way that was domineering toward me. It was a simple move that spoke volumes.

I didn't know where we were going, but I was starting to come to terms with the fact that I enjoyed his presence no matter where we were. And *that* was dangerous territory.

17

ANDREI

I couldn't recall the last time I'd actually been nervous around a woman. I wasn't sure if I ever had been, to be completely honest. The only person who ever made me feel uneasy and nervous was my father. He expected perfection from me in all areas of my life, and if I dissatisfied him? There was nothing my mother could do to interfere in those situations. I just had to grin and bear whatever punishment he deemed was enough for the slight. As a child, I quickly learned that it only got worse if I cried or tried to escape him.

By the time I was thirteen, I was his pride and joy, a trophy to parade around at board meetings. Everyone praised him for raising such a respectful, well-mannered, likely future member of Dracula's board. It was at that same young age that I learned I didn't have a say in my life. It was a never ending punishment, knowing there was nothing I could do to escape his reach. Though, I was very aware I'd break my mother's heart if I ran away and left her alone with him. We were each other's solace and source of warmth in that cold, sterile manor.

When I'd been accepted to the academy years ago, I swore to her I would make my father proud. That I would prove I was worthy of taking over an empty spot on the board should one arise. It wasn't because I gave a shit about him being proud of me. It was because there was no one home for him to take his rage out on besides her if I wasn't there.

At the end of this year, I would accept a position of power, biding my time until a spot emptied on the board, and my father submitted my name to be considered. Not only did I have a track record of obedience, I had also exhibited superior battle prowess at this point. Graduating in the top spot was the final piece of the puzzle I needed to ensure I wouldn't be passed over. Once your name was denied for a position, it could never be submitted again, and I didn't want to see my father's rage if that came to fruition.

Glancing down at the beauty tucked firmly into

my side, I realized my stomach was somersaulting with nerves. I knew I wanted to make her mine, even before I saw her sinking her fingers into her wet cunt. I also knew a woman as powerful as her didn't need anyone at her side, and that fucking scared me. Because while I pictured her at my side, reigning over the world as my queen, I knew she was capable of being one without a king.

Her head tilted up, and I averted my eyes quickly, hoping she didn't realize I'd been staring at her ever since she'd allowed me to wrap my arm around her.

"Are you enjoying the party?" she asked, making easy conversation after we walked far enough away that I'd have to strain pretty damn hard to hear any other conversations.

Dropping my arm from her shoulders, I took a seat on the grass, spreading my legs before tugging her down to sit on the grass between them. I expected her to fight me, but she surprised me, sighing with contentment as she leaned her back against my chest. Tucking her head beneath my chin, I wrapped my arms around her waist and relished the feeling of her warmth pressed against me.

She fit so perfectly in my embrace that I couldn't

help the cringey fucking thought that passed through my mind.. *Maybe she was made for me.*

"The party is okay," I finally answered, offering her a truth I was actually willing to admit aloud. "But I'd rather sit out here under the light of the moon with you than go back."

A rumble of laughter shook her body before she asked, "Is that what you tell all the girls you want to get on their knees for you? It's suave, I'll give you that."

I laughed at her jab before dropping a kiss to the top of her head. "No, baby girl. I've never said anything like that in my life, and I'm pretty sure my reputation would be ruined if you told anyone I said it, so I'm placing a lot of trust in you."

It was a completely fake warning, but I loved joking around with her. It came naturally and filled the space with an easy-going energy I found myself craving. It was light-hearted, which was something I definitely wasn't accustomed to.

She hummed for a second before replying, "We'll see. If you're good tonight, I'll take that secret to my grave. But that's a big if."

A scowl warped my face at the mention of her grave. I didn't want to even joke about it. In fact, I wanted to protect her from the world, and maybe if she allowed me to stay by her side, I could offer her the protection she needed to survive in this world as a slayer turned vampire. I could, and would, use my power as a member of the board to protect her *and* my mother.

Maya had the nerve to corner me after her altercation with Alina in the cafeteria, asking why I wasn't disgusted by what she was. It was honestly a good question, one that had me thinking very seriously about the implications of who and what Alina was in the privacy of my room, right after I'd told Maya to piss off, of course.

The truth was that I accepted that there was nothing Alina could do to prevent herself from being born as a slayer. It was the same reminder that I had to give myself–I couldn't help being born a vampire to the monster who was my father. If I hadn't known my mother's love, I wasn't sure who or what I would have become under his thumb. I didn't know how Alina had come to be a vampire, but I desperately wanted to know more of her story, if simply to begin scratching the surface of who Alina Van Helsing really was. What I knew for certain was that she'd been dragged through hell and broke her chains, claiming her throne for herself. How could I not respect that? Why would her being born a slayer change that?

Slayers and vampires have killed each other for centuries, but it was often the changed vampires–the ones who lost control of themselves with the hunger that overtook them–that gave the rest of us a bad rep with the slayers. After meeting Alina, I had to wonder if it was the same for the slayers who slaughtered innocent vampires just because they could. Had we judged them as a whole because of the atrocities of a few?

I hadn't realized that, while lost in my thoughts, my hands had splayed across her lower abdomen, fingers dangerously close to the apex of her thighs. My nose fell to her throat and I nuzzled into it, pressing a kiss against the side of her neck as she let out a breathy whimper. My cock hardened at the small sound, and I lifted a hand to brush her hair off of her neck, offering me better access to tease the sensitive skin there.

I'd tease her until she was begging for release, and then I'd shove my tongue into her cunt and pinch her clit until she screamed loudly enough for the whole party to hear. It would be the first of many orgasms I planned on giving her now that I was making progress toward claiming her as mine.

"What the fuck?" I growled out as my eyes settled onto the mark on the back of her neck.

It was a small, black drop of blood, signaling she'd found her mate and exchanged blood to seal their bond. It was a mark so many of us yearned for, but the percentage of those who received it was so close to zero it was laughable to call it anything but.

How could she have known she found the one meant for her and still entertained whatever this thing was between us?

Anger blossomed in my vision, seeing red as the telltale signs of the bloodhaze surged forth, gripping me in its clutches.

My hands clenched at my sides tightly as my breathing grew uneven.

How was she not *my* mate? The Fates had to have gotten this wrong. She was everything I needed.

She'd fucking led me on, and I put my heart out there for the first time, genuinely wanting to give her the world.

Jumping to her feet, she whirled around like she was ready to attack someone at my exclamation. Languidly pushing to my feet, I felt the heart that I'd thought dead for so long officially shrivel up in the cavity of my chest.

"How could you?" I hissed.

I had been such a gullible fucking idiot. I thought the Fates had given me what I never knew I needed when she opened that door of the Academic building at the same time I did. Turns out Fate was an arrogant, cold-hearted asshole.

And it turns out Alina was an amazing actress, really laying on her confusion thick to make it seem real. "What are you talking about, Andrei?"

But that was how I'd fallen for her to begin with, wasn't it? I'd given into her act.

"Would you let me sink my fangs into you, too? How far were you going to take this, Alina?" I inquired, genuinely curious about where she'd draw the line in this ploy of hers.

"What makes you think I'd ever let you sink your fangs into me?" she spat the question at me with such venom, that she seemed genuinely confused when I closed the distance between us, eyes widening with shock that I would choose to get so close to her after the warning in her tone.

She took a step back, trying to put distance between us. I didn't allow it, matching each step she took with my much longer stride.

I let out a bone-chilling laugh, gazing down at her through half-lidded eyes. She tipped her chin up in a show of defiance as I lowered my nose to brush against her throat once more, testing her. If she was truly mated, there was no one she would let me pierce her with my fangs. It would be poison in her veins to have someone else's venom running through them.

A shiver ran through her as I whispered against her skin, "What I think is that you'll be screaming my fucking name so loudly the entire school will hear as I sink my fangs into your inner thigh, feasting before giving you an orgasm so intense your mate will come running to defend your honor."

Fuck, despite the revelation of her mate, the thought of feasting on her cunt was still way too appealing. Slowly, I was realizing that there could be an entire empire's worth of space separating us, and the way I burned for her would still consume me. What was it about her that I couldn't walk away from?

I should have left the second I saw the mark. Yet here I was, yearning for the opportunity to challenge her mate for the right to her heart. But when a moan slipped from her parted lips at my dirty words, I realized she wasn't going to admit the truth to me.

Did she think I was an absolute imbecile? Did she forget who the fuck I was?

My chest vibrated against hers with a silent laugh. "I've never hated anyone as much as I hate you for fucking with my emotions like this when you already have a mate," I admitted with a deep, rumbling growl. Inhaling deeply, I let out a shaky breath before adding, "But I never realized how delicious hatred could be until now. Thank you for that, Alina."

At that, she shoved me back, hard. Much harder than I would have thought her capable of, and I went tumbling onto my ass as she darted to stand above me. She dug the bottom of her boot into my chest and demanded, "What the fuck do you mean, I have a mate? Have you lost your ever loving mind?"

Letting my head fall back onto the ground, I let out a humorless laugh, truly astounded she was keeping this up. "Do you think I'm an idiot, Alina? I know what that mark on the back of your neck means. Every vampire knows it's the seal showing that you exchanged blood with your fated mate, sealing your bond."

Her face morphed from one of indignation, to horror, and then quickly to shock.

I wanted to scream at her to give the charade up, but she quickly pulled her boot from my chest and turned, giving me her back.

"Did you ever stop to think that maybe I didn't fucking know? I wasn't raised as a vampire, Andrei, and I sure as shit can't see the back of my neck."

Her voice sounded so damn broken, like she was in true despair at the revelation of the information.

Was she saying she seriously had no idea the mark, about her fated mate?

How was that possible, though? Exchanging blood between vampires wasn't something that just casually happened. It was reserved for the one you knew was yours forever. The rumor was that it heightened things between mates, mentally and physically once complete.

I truly didn't think she was lying now, though, seeing her body language and hearing the anguish in her voice.

Fuck, I was such an ass for jumping to conclusions. Conclusions that didn't match her character at all.

"Who is it, Alina?" I asked, needing to know, though I think a part of me knew the moment I spotted the mark.

I'd seen the possessive way he'd acted around her this morning when I approached her before class started. It had ground his gears to no end to hear our sexually charged conversation.

She took off towards the gate, leaving me behind rather than offering me confirmation, but I knew it was Lincoln, and I was going to kill that motherfucker for bonding to her without her knowing the implications. Not to mention the way he treated her like trash by ensuring every damn vampire in our sector knew who she was, was absolutely fucking unacceptable.

He'd written the expiration date of her life with that, and I was going to ensure I did the same for him.

Maybe at the end of all that, Alina would find it within her to forgive me for assuming the worst of the situation. I wasn't going to hold my breath, though. I'd fucked up, and she didn't seem to be the forgiving type.

18

ALINA

Prior to last night, I thought I understood what it meant to operate on autopilot. I thought I knew coldness and how to handle dissociating from my emotions. But the way the hours slogged by through my Praeditus 101 and Diplomacy classes today, through Andrei pleading with me to have a moment of my time to talk about last night, and through Maya and Milina trying to get a rise out of me in the cafeteria...I realized that *this* was the absolute rock bottom.

Never in my life had I felt so...empty. I'd even sunk as low as to put on the blazer and skirt provided for me, not bothering to give a shit about what clothes I covered myself with today.

There was no rage to keep me afloat and fighting.

Last night and all day today, my thoughts were tangled in the implications of what happened with Lincoln and I. We were supposedly mates, ones who had sealed our bond according to Andrei. I'd been in disbelief at first, but as I laid in my bed all night thinking about it, restless and exhausted all at once, I realized it made perfect sense.

The way I'd felt Lincoln's emotions and heard his thoughts before it had abruptly cut off...The way our necks burned simultaneously...It all added up.

And I fucking hated that it made sense. Because Lincoln elicited exactly two responses from me: desire to have him around for the rest of my life as a partner who challenged me appropriately, or disgust at the realization that I was better off without him. I couldn't see how we could ever bridge this emotional chasm between us, to provide an environment where a real relationship could flourish, one where we wouldn't continue to feed the toxicity we'd cultivated in such a short time.

There were moments I was convinced of the truth behind his concern for my well-being, but there were moments where I was more convinced by his disgust for who I truly was.

I didn't even know what this bond meant. How would it impact me? Did I have to remain with him? Would it disrupt my future plans?

So many questions whirled through my mind, completely obscuring what was going on in real time around me. Thankfully, with so many students hungover in two classes full of textbook reading and assignments, the day seemed docile in comparison to the ones before it.

My pen scratched over the paper as I finished filling in the last prompt on the page for my Diplomacy assignment. With a quiet groan, I got up, grabbing my bag and stalking toward the front of the class to drop the assignment into the designated bin in front of the professor before taking my leave of the class. I had mentor training in the combat room in roughly thirty minutes, which was just enough time to snag a few bags of blood to refuel and make it back to the room.

I wasn't sure exactly what the training would entail or who it was with, but I hoped I would be able to regain some iota of my anger over what was happening in my life. I hated walking around like I wasn't even present in my body. What was worse was knowing I felt that way and feeling utterly incapable of snapping myself out of it.

Entering the dorm house, I headed for my usual fridge, faltering in the archway of the room as I saw Maya leaning against it with a smug smirk of satisfaction on her face. I didn't have it in me to play her games today, so I turned on my heel to head to my room, but stopped as her voice rang out behind me.

"What, are you afraid of me now? Or did you realize Andrei was just playing with you and came to visit my room last night after the party ended?"

It was like she'd attached jumper cables to my heart, turned the ignition, and revved the gas, kick-starting my emotions with her questions.

Fury coursed through my body, fiery and uncontrolled, at the idea of him in her room, doing everything he promised he'd do to my body. His face buried between her legs and her moans echoing through the air.

My vision tinged red as I let out a feral scream, shooting back toward her, not giving a shit about who was around. Grabbing her shoulders, I slammed her body into the fridge and, smiling with satisfaction as the metal creaked and gave way under the force of her body impacting into it. The impact reverberated, rattling through my bones as I yelled, "What the fuck did you just say?"

Her lips curled back in a smile, and I acted on

instinct, smashing my forehead into her fucking nose. The cartilage crushed beneath the blow, and as I pulled back, blood flowed down her face and lined her teeth. She snarled, "You fucking heard me. He fucked me until the sun came up, you filthy bitch."

It was odd, the way my rage calmed, like a tornado evaporating after miles of destruction. Silence, cool and collected settled over me as I stared at the pathetic woman in front of me. As she snarled at me through her bloody mouth, I felt the truth of the situation deep within my damn soul: Andrei wouldn't do that.

He wouldn't fucking touch her, and she and I both knew that. For once, I'd let her get to me.

Letting out a heavy sigh, I let her go and stepped back, curling my lip in disgust. "You're pathetic, Maya. Move on and find someone who actually gives a shit about you."

I turned, taking a step away from her but paused when pain lanced through my scalp. Maya's fingers wrapped through my hair, and she pulled a chunk of my hair back harshly, preventing me from leaving while I still had any semblance of control. I was so fucking done with this situation, like so fucking done. All I could do was wrack my brain, trying to think up the quickest way to get out of this shitshow without any more back and forth.

Turning toward her, I wound my arm back and tucked my fingers into a fist before letting it fly towards her head. The punch landed perfectly on her temple, and she crumpled, fingers loosening around her grip on my hair as she hit the ground like a rag doll.

Gasps sounded from the students nearest us; and as I yanked open the crushed fridge door to get a few bags of blood, I announced loudly over the creaking of the metal, "Someone let this bitch know I'm tired of kicking her ass. I'm actually starting to feel bad about it."

I strolled at a languid pace towards the combat room, not willing to be within the same four walls as Maya when she woke up. Unfortunately for me, I stepped toward the building at the same moment Andrei was finishing his assignment for strategy. I halted in my path, not willing to look him in the eyes after I'd just lost my shit on Maya for what she'd said about him.

I knew he'd find out the second he walked into the dorms, but fuck me, I didn't want to have to own up to it right now. It would show him I gave a shit about what he did—or *who* he did, and I wasn't fully ready to accept that.

When I'd been settled between his legs last night and tucked into his embrace, for a moment, all of my concerns surrounding Lincoln and life in general had faded away. Andrei had provided me a moment of peace I wasn't sure I'd ever feel again. He'd felt like home. For a split second, it felt like I wasn't me acting alone against the rest of the damn world.

And then he'd assumed the worst of me without even asking a few quick questions that would have cleared up the situation instantly. He could have provided me some much needed information while offering a great moment for open dialogue between us too. Instead, he showed me his true colors and a nasty side of him that reminded me too much of Lincoln.

It seemed I was the queen of being drawn to men who were just as fucked up as I was inside. There was no path to happiness for anyone who couldn't process their trauma and heal. None of us were even remotely close to that.

As soon as he shot toward me, I took off as well, narrowly avoiding him as we rushed by each other. I didn't stop until I was in the building, zipping down the hallway to the combat classroom. Throwing the door open, I took a breath of relief as the darkness of the room swallowed me whole. Sliding down the wall, I placed my bags of blood on the ground and drained them one by one until my stomach felt full.

After a long stretch of silence, where I found myself contemplating how the fuck I was going to keep going on like this, I realized I wasn't alone in the room. My stomach tightened as I spotted Lincoln's figure dropping off of the obstacle course and prowling toward me. He wore tight shorts, and nothing else, and was absolutely drenched in sweat, as if he'd been pushing himself all damn day.

Because of course he had to be here, and of course my fucking hormones were turning into whore-moans, focusing on how damn delectable he looked despite my extreme disappointment in him.

My heart raced erratically, and I hated how my eyes narrowed in on the single bead of sweat rolling down his jaw before it dripped down to the soft flesh of his neck. His pulse thrummed steadily beneath the bead of liquid, and my fangs ached to be released. To sink into his throat and drink his blood from him.

To let it roll over my tongue and spill down my

throat as the endorphins spurred us both on in the heat of the moment.

Drinking his blood hadn't gone well the first time, so I sure as fuck didn't know why I was craving it now.

I needed to get the hell out of this room and far, far away from him. Pushing myself to my feet with the intention of leaving, I barely took a step toward the door before he appeared in front me a few paces away, blocking my path.

"Stop running from your problems, Alina," he growled, and my mind jumbled, signals crossing between wanting to fuck him and wanting to murder him.

Fuck this. *Fuck him.*

Bold of him to say, as someone who quite literally ran from our problem the other night.

Shaking my head, I clucked my tongue a couple times before glancing into the burning red embers of his eyes. The beast within him was fully in control. Not a glimmer of hazel remained behind.

"Maybe save your advice for those who ask for it, bud," I snapped and bared my fangs that had elongated in my rage.

For a second, I was shocked at the silence that followed my statement. His eyes focused on me like a predator stalking its prey, but the subtle tick of his jaw let me know that my words did get to him.

He was still for a moment after his jaw tensed, but then he made his move. My hair blew back as he launched toward me, pinning me against the wall before I could react. Wriggling my body and thrashing my arms, I tried to break free but to no avail. Lincoln's body was pressed so tightly to me there was no room to gain the momentum needed to help me break out.

He was stronger than me, but one day that wouldn't be the case. I'd be stronger than all of them, and I'd never let anyone I loved be hurt by them ever again.

I'd never be hurt by them again.

So why did my body love the feeling of being trapped against his as his chest heaved, pressing against my breasts?

My breath caught in my throat as he lowered his nose to my neck, nudging the vein that was pounding with the beat of my overworked heart. When I tried to kick out with my legs, he took the opportunity to nudge his corded, muscular thigh between my legs, pressing it against my heat in a way that pulled a gasp from me as sparks danced in my eyes.

This was wrong.

So fucking wrong.

He was my enemy and my teacher.

He was also my mate.

His lips brushed my skin delicately, the feeling at odds with his menacing whisper, "I'm not your bud. Don't ever call me that again."

I couldn't help myself. A scoff burst from my mouth as I retorted, "I'll call you whatever the *fuck* I want, bud."

Why did I want to challenge him, to feel the full extent of his wrath? Why was I even entertaining whatever the fuck this was with him? I couldn't control myself around him. He just pulled this primal side out of me.

Lincoln's hand darted up, wrapping around my throat, and my head tilted back on instinct as my eyes fluttered closed. A breathy moan escaped my half-parted lips as his fingers tightened on me. His thigh pressed into me further, and I had to bite my bottom lip so hard that I felt the sting of my fangs slicing it open in order to keep myself grounded and to keep me from grinding against him in pleasure.

His sharp intake of breath was the first reminder that I fucked up by spilling my blood in front of him again. The second reminder was when his head jerked up and his mouth descended onto mine.

I was instantly lost under his touch, opening on instinct and clashing my tongue with his as my blood swirled between us. He groaned and I pushed into him further, needing more. Needing all of him.

It was fucking euphoria.

No. *No.*

I would not lose myself to whatever this so-called fated mate bullshit was just because this infuriating vampire caused my pussy to throb with a desire I'd never, ever experienced before.

As his tongue darted out and lapped up the blood still streaming from my lip, I did the only thing I could think of to break the tension of the moment. My hand cracked against his cheek, the sound echoing through the empty room.

I opened my eyes to see the still-red vortex of his eyes gazing back at me. A second later, he snatched my wrists with one hand and pinned them against the wall above my head. It was a painfully hard grip, but I would be lying if I said I didn't enjoy the bite of the pain.

Cocking his head to the side, his voice dropped to a husky whisper as he ran his thumb along my bottom lip roughly, "Don't try that again, Spitfire."

Fates, I wanted to try it again. So badly.

But part of me also wondered how incredible it would feel to give into this completely, even if just for one night. Maybe all I needed was to get it out of my system one good time to properly clear my head.

There was still so much to talk about, but my body signaled to my brain that the time for talking was over. I wanted to see if his bark matched his bite, now.

19

LINCOLN

Hatred had a specific taste.

It was bitter and pungent, yet somehow you found yourself craving the repulsive taste of it. It bred desperation in a way you'd never known. Once you had your first taste, it became an addiction that snaked its way up your spine and took root.

I'd finally realized I didn't hate Alina, though. I hated what she represented as the ghost of my trauma from childhood.

Alina...she was mine.

I had been an absolute bastard for throwing up a mental shield and high-tailing it out of there when I'd realized she could hear my thoughts. The way I'd been raised, it was frowned upon to show emotions.

It left you exposed and showed your enemies exactly how to take you down. Despite being out of that rigid lifestyle for so long, it still seemed to be ingrained in my psyche, making it my knee-jerk reaction.

I'd been so damn angry with the Fates at first. I couldn't comprehend why they would make a slayer my mate after everything I'd been through. But as the night had dragged on, and despite the distance stretching between us, flickers of her emotions and thoughts came through.

She'd been elated to find Andrei, and he'd brought out a plethora of emotions that only I should provoke from her. She'd run right into his arms because of how I'd reacted, and it was a hell like no other I'd ever experienced to know she was meant for me but was finding solace with another. I could blame no one for it but myself.

She hadn't known to put up a mental barrier, and even if she had, I wasn't sure she knew how. Catching bits and pieces of her thoughts and feelings was agony; though from what I'd found in my reading about mates from years past, the further you were from each other, the harder it was to get a clear read on the shared conscious state you were gifted after completing the bond. Even across miles,

I'd felt her hatred for me rip across the bond we shared. I'd felt her desperation as she clung to Andrei. I'd felt her heartbreak when he'd hurt her too.

As my finger brushed roughly across her bottom lip, her tongue darted out to lick it teasingly.

I couldn't tell whether she was actually into this moment or if she was trying to arouse me as a ploy to escape.

A deep rumble ripped from my chest as my eyes tracked the movement of her tongue. The sound seemed to embolden her, and she parted her lips, sucking my thumb into the wet heat of her mouth and swirling her tongue around it like I wanted her to do to my cock.

I had tried to act like I was unaffected by her since meeting her Sunday, but fuck me, my Spitfire owned me. I couldn't deny it any longer, and the holes in my wall from my rage at her being with Andrei was a stark reminder that, though I awoke this morning trying to figure out how to fix what I'd broken between us, I was the one who broke us.

She was livid with Andrei for accusing her of playing him, and she'd been avoiding him since last night. It brought me a weird sense of calm, knowing he'd fucked up too. I could take her being pissed at both of us. I couldn't stand him being in her good graces when I wasn't.

If I would have thought with my brain and not my cock last night, I'd have stopped us from sharing blood. The tension between us had risen to a stifling level that made me want to scream right until the moment we'd finally given into temptation and kissed. It was undoubtedly the most magnificent moment of my life, feeling the softness of her lips against mine as she sank into my embrace, bodies melded. It was so much better than my imagination had conjured, and all logic flew out the window.

There was so much I would change about last night, but the biggest part was how she'd found out from someone else about the depth of what we were to each other. She had every right to hate me, to be disappointed in me. I couldn't blame her because I felt the exact same way with myself.

If she would rather face the sexual tension between us first, though, I wasn't going to stop her. I needed her so fucking badly, and now that it was confirmed we were mates, the ethics of my position at the academy didn't matter. A mate bond was above any rules or laws in Sanguis and Dark Imaginarium Academy.

She peeked up at me coyly from beneath her

dark lashes, and batted them twice, daring me to make a move. I snapped, giving into my carnal urges and letting go of the last semblance of control I had over the rigid tension I'd carried around her at all times.

Pressing my finger further into her mouth, my cock hardened painfully when she eagerly opened her mouth and stuck her tongue out for me.

"Such a good girl," I praised before shoving it to the back of her throat, making her gag on it and loving the way tears pricked her eyes instantly. I didn't relent though, wanting—no, needing— to see if she'd back down. I had to know her boundaries.

She whimpered, but I couldn't tell if it was from pleasure or pain, so I swiftly pulled my finger out of her mouth, moving my hand to tangle tightly into the hair at the nape of her neck instead. She sucked in a deep breath of air as I yanked her head back, lowering my chin so my stubble scratched against the sensitive skin of her neck. I inhaled her scent deeply, trying to commit it to memory before slowly dragging my tongue over the area I'd just scraped my chin against.

This felt almost too good to be true, us both deciding to give into the desire blazing between us at the same time. Fear existed deep within me. Fear that, despite her fire and bratty tendencies, I would push her too far with my needs and my plans to satisfy them.

Placing my lips against the shell of her ear, I whispered, "I don't know the ending to our story yet. All I know is that for this chapter, I want you on your fucking knees, Princess."

Please, don't let her stare at me in disgust.

"I'm not asking for forever," she answered in a breathy voice I hardly recognized. "I'm asking you to make me forget about the rest of the world while it's just you and me in these four walls."

We'd have to work on that whole not asking for forever thing. It kind of came with the territory of being mates, but now wasn't the time to push her.

She didn't move to her knees, despite my request. Instead, she ran her tongue across her top lip slowly and purposefully. Shooting me a wink, she challenged, "I don't get on my knees for just any man. So you'll have to make me, *Sir*."

So, she wanted me to get a little forceful. Fuck, the Fates really made her for me.

My eyes blazed with lust at her words, and in the span of my next breath, the cold edge of the knife I kept in a pocket at all times was pressed to her throat. The metal gleamed over the steady pulse that thrummed blood through the carotid artery beneath it.

Her legs shifted together, thighs gripping the muscles in my own leg as she twisted her hips, trying to get friction. She fucking loved the danger. She craved it, and I could give it to her. I could provide the safe place for her to give up her control she so desperately wanted stripped away.

It was a heavy burden to carry, being in control all the time. I understood that all too well, and it just so happened that we had opposing ways of giving it up, allowing us to both get what we needed right now. I drew out my next words slowly, and with purpose.

"Get. On. Your. Fucking. Knees. Princess."

Still, she didn't relent, glaring at me in a challenging way that read, "I dare you," like she thought I wouldn't knick that pretty skin of hers. How had she forgotten so quickly that I loved to see her bleed for me?

I pressed the knife against her skin, and her breathing grew erratic, eyes dilating to pinpricks as she felt a sting of pain kissed with pleasure. Her eyes fluttered in what seemed like a mixture of relief and bliss as she slid away from my thigh, finally sinking to her knees.

Was she actually relieved that I would go so far to challenge her?

I'd always thought something was wrong with me, with the way I wanted to dominate her until she had no choice but to submit to me. The truth was, though, that in a power dynamic like ours, she wasn't truly submitting to me. She was allowing me to have the power, entrusting me to take care of her needs and ensure her safety through it, all while maintaining a solid hold on her own agency.

We were equals, no matter what it seemed like from the outside.

Dropping to a crouch, I ripped the front of her blazer open with my knife in a succinct move, causing buttons to fly in every direction and leaving her in nothing but a black, lace bra. I didn't speak, interested to see if she had anything to say to me instead, but she simply gazed back at me with beautiful red eyes that no doubt matched my own.

The tip of my knife pressed into her lower stomach, and I dragged it upward ever so slowly with a feather-light kiss of pressure until it rested in the valley of her breasts. Without warning, I flipped it sideways and tore the knife down and out, cutting the middle of her bra open and exposing her breasts to me.

"I'm not a man who deserves this, Princess," I growled as I stood to my full height and took in her state of undress.

I was entranced by her, completely absorbed within the powerful, confident energy she somehow still exuded, even from her knees.

I flicked the small blade back into its sheath before tossing my knife to the ground. I heaved a deep breath, calming my racing heart as I commanded her, "Open your mouth for me, Princess."

Her eyes fluttered closed as a small moan bubbled from her lips at my words.

Yes. Fuck yes.

She truly was my match.

Maybe we were twin flames that needed an escape from the skeletons from our past waiting for us on the other side of these four walls. Maybe we could go up in fucking flames together, forgetting about our pasts in this moment of solitude.

Hooking my fingers into the waistband of my shorts, I dropped them to the floor and walked forward until my cock bobbed in front of her slightly ajar mouth. Letting out a chuckle of amusement for how she thought that barely parted mouth was going to accommodate my girth, I instructed, "Relax your jaw and open as wide as you can."

She did as I asked, and I lowered my hips until my tip pressed into the wet heat of her mouth. She closed her lips around me, flicking her tongue up and over my glistening pre-cum, humming in delight.

That single sound unraveled me entirely. I couldn't be gentle with her.

Growling lightly, I tangled my hand back into her hair, pulling her head back until a new angle allowed my cock further access to her throat as I sank deeper into her. Tears welled in her eyes as she struggled to take me. I was only halfway in, and I didn't plan on letting her out of this until I hit the back of her throat.

As I began to rock my hips, fucking her throat slowly to allow her time to acclimate to my size, I praised her. "You are doing so fucking well, Princess. I'm going to push back further and you need to swallow me down, okay?"

Tears poured from her eyes as she looked up at me from beneath wet lashes and attempted to nod. Sliding all the way back with one thrust, her eyes popped open as she swallowed and I sank down perfectly.

Fucking hell, I was about to blow my load just at the sight of my cock bulging in her throat.

She began struggling, and I ran an affectionate hand through her hair before fisting it and instructing, "Breathe through your nose, Princess. That's so good."

My body felt like it was on fire, and my knees trembled as I felt my balls tightening, seeking release. I saw her hand snake down to play with her pussy beneath her skirt, and it pulled a possessive snarl from me. "This is mine, Princess," I stated. "You come when I let you."

She moaned at my words but dragged her hand away from her pussy, instead lifting it up to cup my balls and roll them slightly. And then I let go, fucking her mouth until I saw stars and exploded down her throat.

Waiting just long enough to ensure she swallowed every drop, I pulled from her mouth and wrapped my hand around her throat. She let out a small yelp of surprise as I forced her onto her back before pulling her legs up enough to slide underneath them, hooking them over my shoulders as I settled my face under her skirt and against her thong. With a frustrated growl at the offending material being in the way of my meal, I let my fangs come down and ripped into them, tearing the front and exposing her completely.

Letting out a rumble of contentment, my tongue flicked out to tease her clit and immediately her legs tightened around my neck, spurring me on. Flattening my tongue, I placed more pressure on her sensitive bundle of swollen nerves and settled into a frenzied pace. I was rewarded with a quick cry of pleasure from her, and I growled against her pussy, needing more of her sounds.

She'd been such a good girl, I couldn't fail to make sure she got her reward.

She grew slicker with arousal, and I forced her right leg up to allow my arm room to move. Positioning two fingers at her entrance, I began to suck on her clit as I plunged them into her. Her walls clenched around me in a vice-like grip as her hips bucked and she cried out, "Lincoln, fuck yes."

Somehow my cock was already hardening, readying for round two at the sound of those three words spilling breathily from her lips.

Alternating between sucking and flicking my tongue against her clit, I slipped a third finger in, stretching her fully. I needed to acclimate her before sinking my cock into her in the future. Curling my fingers deep into her and stroking, I felt her body trembling, already on the precipice of shattering for me. I pulled my face back just enough to command, "Come all over my fingers and face, Princess."

She cried my name once more before her pussy spasmed. I lifted my head up, knocking her skirt back as I continued to stroke her until she came, soaking the floor and bringing a pleased smirk to my face.

Her cheeks were flushed, and I saw her fingers pinching her nipples in the seconds before her hands fell to the side, thumping against the floor as her chest heaved with deep breaths. Slipping my fingers out of her, I gathered her into my arms and held her, hoping we could just bask in the moment of closeness for a few more minutes.

"Lincoln," she murmured, an adorably drowsy tone accompanying my name.

Running my fingers through her hair, I held her tighter and whispered, "I know. We'll talk, I promise, Princess."

I knew I'd get on my fucking knees and beg for her forgiveness at this point. I couldn't walk away from her or our bond ever again.

After a few minutes, I set her down and grabbed

her blazer, helping her put it back on. "Hold it closed," I instructed as I tossed her ripped bra in the trash can near the door.

She did as I requested, still in the mood to listen to me, which felt like a fucking miracle. After pulling my shorts back on, I swept her back into my arms before speeding to the dorm house. Her head lolled against my chest, her small hand splayed against my abdomen, and I swear some of the darkness around my heart began to flake away.

It felt so damn good to hold her in my arms, to not be arguing with her for once. I think I would always crave our banter and challenging energy the way I sometimes craved blood because it made these moments of peace that much more special.

Flying up the stairs to the top floor, I turned left and quickly opened my door before shutting it behind us. As I approached the edge of my bed, I leaned down with the intention of letting her get comfortable there, but her hands flew around my neck, holding me against her.

"Don't let go yet," she pleaded, and I swallowed thickly, my throat clogged with emotion.

How much of a bastard was I for making her think I would leave her again? She clung to me, prolonging what she thought was inevitable. *Fuck.*

“Prin...” I started, but paused when I realized that particular pet name only fit her in specific scenarios. I let go of her legs, letting her fall to her knees on the mattress so she faced me with her arms wrapped around my neck. I snaked an arm around the small of her back, tugging her firmly to me. Placing my other hand on the back of her head, I took a deep breath and tried again, “Spitfire, I’m not going anywhere ever again, and I’m so fucking sorry my actions have made you think that’s what I’ll always do. I know it’s my fault, but please let me prove to you that it can change.”

Gingerly, her grip on my neck loosened and she pulled back to look into my eyes, searching to see if I was being genuine, I’m sure. Vulnerability shone brightly in her silver eyes as she whispered, “I don’t know if I can let someone in again. I can’t handle the agony of losing someone I care about...” she trailed off, tears slipping down her cheeks.

I wanted to punish myself for planning her expulsion from the academy, despite knowing she had nowhere to go if she wasn’t here. I’d been able to deduce she’d been turned against her will with that statement. The slayers would never let her stay, and with her visceral hatred of vampires, she wouldn’t settle in Sanguis either.

There was something deeper to her words, though–a pain buried so deep that with the bond we shared, the weight of her loss hit me like a bag of bricks and knocked the breath from me. Somehow she'd managed to throw up a mental shield when she recognized me in the combat room, and I could only assume it was a natural reaction to being pissed at me and wanting to get away. But with each passing moment, it grew weaker, letting her emotions spill out, though her thoughts remained her own.

"You won't lose me," I whispered back, brushing her tears from her cheeks. "This bond between us? It's forever. You could run away from me, but it wouldn't change the fact that our souls are destined to be entwined."

Her throat bobbed as she swallowed before murmuring, "But what about you being my professor? How can we possibly give this a chance?"

Relief barreled through me, and I was able to truly smile with the knowledge that her fear was unfounded. She didn't know our laws, it seemed, and for the first time I could ease her fears rather than adding to them. "In Sanguis, and at Dark Imaginarium Academy, fated mate bonds supersede all ethics and laws. No one, besides us, can keep us apart, Spitfire."

"Oh," she breathed out, and I felt tension easing from her body as I held her. "I didn't expect it to be that simple."

Leaning forward to press my lips to her forehead, I admitted, "It's the only time I'll accept the easy path with you."

Her soft laughter made my heart soar, and I shifted us to lay on the bed together, loving the way she immediately curled around me. As my mind began to drift into a sleepy haze, exhausted from how hard I'd pushed myself today as I worked through my emotions, I heard her whisper, "You're still a jerk."

My lips curled up in a smirk, chest shaking with barely-contained laughter. "I know, Spitfire."

I would get her up so we could both shower soon, but for now, we both seemed content to lay together, processing this monumental step forward for us.

"I hope one day you'll trust me enough to share the burdens you're carrying around," I admitted, pulling her face to rest against the crook of my chest and shoulder. "I'd fight away all of your fears and the demons from your past if you asked me to, but I know you don't need me to do that for you. So, I'll be here, however you'll have me."

Silence stretched between us as she traced swirls over my chest with the tip of her finger.

"One day," she murmured before taking a deep inhale of breath, exhaling the rest of her sentence with a heavy sigh, "I'll share with you."

Her promise, the guarantee that there would be a future, was enough for me to close my eyes, feeling at peace for the first time since childhood.

Fates, don't let me fuck this up. I knew she wouldn't give me another chance if I did, and I didn't want to try living without her again.

20

ALINA

Nerves bunched in my stomach as my hand settled on the door of my room. Despite feeling like we had so much to talk about, the ease of that simple moment we'd shared in his bed wiped away a lot of my fears in regards to Lincoln. I hadn't been able to stop myself from latching onto him when he tried to put me down on his bed, as if my body suddenly realized it needed him more than my brain cared to admit.

So much for distancing myself from my emotions. Had I even really committed to not letting them control my decisions?

The visceral fear of him leaving me again, even in such a minor way, had turned my stomach leaden, filled with despair. Logically, I knew I would be fine without him—but I was realizing I didn't want to be. We showered and laid together, allowing ourselves to soak in the other's presence without a blanket of sexual tension smothering us for the first time. During our time together, he'd explained the way the bond allowed us to hear each other's thoughts and emotions when there wasn't a mental shield in place.

I'd been surprised when he worked with me to fortify mine until it was solid. I'd figured he wanted to hear and feel every damn detail that was going on in my body. I couldn't help the sinking feeling in my gut at the realization that he'd heard, or maybe even felt, strong emotions about Andrei on the night of the party, and I struggled to reconcile the fact that he was *still* willing to help me fortify my shields, granting me privacy from him. He didn't bring up the surge of emotion attached to Andrei, though, so I let it go for now.

With a huff of air falling through my lips, I opened my door, steeling myself for what today might bring. Andrei, coincidentally, was the exact reason I was dreading today. Lincoln and I agreed to remain professional in classes, but I wasn't sure we were going to be able to completely hide the progression of our relationship.

The thought of Andrei seeing the change in my relationship with our professor broke my heart. Because at the end of the day, I felt the same exact fucking pull to him that I felt toward Lincoln. What was I supposed to do about it now that I was mated, though? I had these feelings for Andrei before I bonded with Lincoln, but that didn't stop it from feeling like cheating now. I couldn't just poof away the undeniable pull I felt to him.

I was still pissed as hell that he'd assumed such poor things about my character, but one of the most important lessons I was learning here was that we were all capable of making mistakes in heated moments. Andrei possessed the emotional intelligence to quickly realize the error of his ways; and when I stood back to look at it subjectively, I could understand why he reacted so viscerally after seeing the mark.

No one here was used to being around a vampire who wasn't fully entrenched in their culture.

When I'd come to the academy, finding a mate had never been a blip on my radar. But here I was, days in, mated and still pining after another. Seriously, I wasn't sure how Queen Ama managed it with her eight mates. The amount of testosterone alone...that was a hard pass from me. I would drown if one more man walked into my life.

Knowing I promised Lincoln I would be a little early to class for a moment of privacy, I raced to the cafeteria to grab some bags to go. I skidded into the cafeteria, stomach gnawing for sustenance, but horror washed over me when I found the fridge with animal blood completely empty.

No. *No.* I couldn't drink human blood.

I needed to find Lincoln immediately. He'd know what happened to the supply and could likely help me find access to my preferred blood.

I turned on my heel, making a beeline for the classroom, the world rushing by in a blur with my burst of speed. Flinging the door open, I yelled, "Lincoln! We have a—" but broke off when I took in the scene before me.

He was locked into a battle with Andrei, whose fury seeped through the room. The fury was a noxious, palpable thing, grabbing hold of me and riling my own emotions. Fuck, I needed to feed. I knew their fight was likely about me, and I would absolutely address the issues with them both after I got some damn blood in me.

It was almost impossible to track them as they tossed each other across the room before pouncing back on their opponent. Fists and elbows flew around, blood splattering over the mats as they tussled.

My lips thinned as I tried to think of what to do. Unsure of Andrei's power or battle prowess, I wasn't sure if I was ready to fight him. But I knew for a fact that Lincoln was a hell of a lot stronger than me. If I did insert myself into the middle of it, I didn't think either of them would intentionally hurt me, but I doubted my ability to put an end to it.

What would break their concentration?

A thought sprang to my mind immediately, and I pinched the bridge of my nose, shaking my head at the shit my brain conjured up in the heat of the moment. But you know what? *Fuck it.* I didn't have time for this shit, and if this is what it took to get me my blood quickly, I wasn't ashamed, just maybe a little stupid.

I'd settled on black jeans and a new blazer today, not wanting to flash anyone my ass in combat. Seriously, why were skirts even part of our uniform? I shook the unhelpful away and made quick work of the blazer's buttons before letting it drop to the floor in a heap. I kicked my shoes off before dragging my hands toward the button on my jeans.

Hooking my fingers in the waistband of the

jeans, I rolled my eyes at the stupidity of men. There were way more important things at hand here, and they wanted to have a dick-measuring contest? Growling, I decided to try reasoning with them, though I was doubtful it would work. "If you guys are done with your early morning brawl, I really need help locating some animal blood. The fridge in the cafeteria was empty."

When they didn't stop, my blood boiled, anger pulsed through my veins, hot and insistent. I raged silently as they brawled, taking a moment to really let their idiocy wash over me. My fists clenched and unclenched at my sides, and by the time I was screaming at the top of my lungs, the anger tinged the edges of my vision red. "I'M NAKED!"

I wasn't fully naked, having kept my bra and underwear on, but they didn't need to know those details when I'd announced my nudity. After all, a girl had to keep it classy, not trashy, but just a little bit nasty.

It was fucking laughable, the way in which they both came to a stop, Lincoln hovering with his fist inches away from Andrei's face as they both stared over at me.

These fucking *idiots*.

What was even more amusing was how quickly

they both managed to make it to my side, grabbing my clothes and shoving them at me.

"He does not deserve to see you like that," they said in unison, and my hunger faded into the back of my mind as I bent at the waist, cackling.

Honestly, I shouldn't have laughed, but it was just so fucking funny how they were acting like they were defending my honor, when I was the one who stripped down on purpose. No one held a gun to my head to make me. And at the end of the day, the action had the intended effect. Even if it was stupid.

When I saw Lincoln taking a step toward Andrei, I snapped out of it. I didn't have time for their pissing contest. "Hey, stop!" I exclaimed, stepping between them and placing a hand on each of their chests as they loomed over me.

"Lincoln, there is no animal blood for me," I barked out, but he continued to push against my hand, snarling in Andrei's direction. "Do you even hear me? You know I won't drink human blood."

I craned my head back, begging the asshole to just listen to me. After a moment, his lashes fluttered, blinking a few times with clarity as he processed my words. I breathed a sigh of relief at the sight of the red tinge fading from his eyes.. "Are you sure? That's impossible. They stock it every morning and if there's going to be a shortage of anything, they try to give us a warning ahead of time in order to wean the vampire off the item."

"Yes, I'm sure. I need blood before class starts, unless we want a repeat of me losing myself as I pummeled Maya into the ground."

"To be fair," Andrei said, "with your track record, there's a pretty good chance you might still do that, even with a full stomach."

The mirth in his voice eased some of the tension lining my body, and I felt my shoulders sag lightly. I sent a playful wink his way, thankful that whatever the fuck was happening between them was at least on the backburner for now.

"Shhhhh," I voiced as I held a finger to his lips briefly.

Lincoln let out a grunt, pacing in front of me as he looked at the clock on the wall above the door. "Class is about to start. I don't have time to go to the academic building and see what is going on with the animal blood right now."

"I can go," Andrei offered easily, shrugging his shoulders. "Just give me a hall pass or some shit, Lincoln."

Lincoln's fangs popped out and his chest puffed up, "It's Professor Aldea to you, and just so we're perfectly fucking clear, I am more than capable of taking care of my mate."

I quickly saw where this was going so I snatched my clothes from them, yanking them on and huffing in annoyance the whole time. "While you two continue your pissing match, I'll go to the academic building myself to figure it out. Have fun."

I was finishing the last button on my blazer, glaring my annoyance at the men staring at me with slack-jawed expressions, when I heard Estrid's voice coming from down the hallway. My eyes darted toward Lincoln in confusion. "Do you think she's here to talk to us about that now?" It seemed odd that she would be, but they were close enough that the headmistress might make a visit over something like this.

Both Lincoln's and Andrei's faces paled as they exchanged looks of concern, which only served to confuse me further. Two minutes ago they were ready to tear each other's throats out, and now they're sharing concern over something? Bizarre. Absolutely fucking bizarre.

"Linc–" I started, but cut off at the sound of another voice alongside Estrid's.

It was deep and sultry, and the velvety tone caused a shiver of anticipation to race down my spine. I couldn't lie, the man could've cracked open a thesaurus to read, and I would have given the performance a five out of five stars. There was something gravely, with an underlying lilt of seduction about the tone that just...did it for me.

"What's going on?" I hissed at the men, who had gone still as statues.

"That's..." Andrei started, but he was cut off as the man appeared in the doorway, his presence choking silence into the room.

His ebony hair was slicked back with longer hair resting on the top and the sides shaved shorter. A sharp, three-piece suit fit him like a glove, and the cologne he wore wafted into the room, making my nostrils flare as I scented him. To top it off, he had a perfectly trimmed dark beard that added this more edgy vibe to his ensemble. Everything about him screamed money, power, and sex.

"Dracula," he said, filling in the blank for Andrei. He smirked, exposing his fangs. "Pleasure to make your acquaintance, Ms..."

Dracula.

That was *Dracula*.

My body had gone into a catatonic state, incapable of computing his sudden arrival.

"This is Ms. Alina Van Helsing," Estrid provided

when I couldn't seem to make my brain and mouth work together to give him my name. There was pride in her tone and a smile lighting up her face as she winked at me.

Fuck.

21

ALINA

Estrid had no idea what Dracula really meant to me. All she knew was that I'd asked if it was possible to get a job working for him at the end of my time at the academy. Sweet, sweet, Estrid. She probably thought meeting him would make my whole day, if not year.

I waited for the cold, calculated look to enter his eyes when her words sank in. For him to realize I was the little play toy he'd used in some grand scheme that I couldn't possibly understand the extent of.

But it never came.

Instead, he walked over and offered me his hand to shake as a perfect smile graced his handsome face. "A true pleasure, Ms. Van Helsing."

There was no bitterness or malicious undertone to his words. The fucker sounded genuine, making me wonder what game he was playing at. Deciding to play it right back, I placed my hand into his outstretched one, shaking it as rage coursed through my body. He shifted quickly, bringing the top of my hand toward his lips and brushed them over my knuckles with a feather light kiss.

What the actual fuck is going on right now?

I could almost feel Lincoln and Andrei bristling at the gesture, and I watched as Dracula's eyes swept in their direction, not missing their reactions either. As he dropped my hand and clasped his own behind his back, he hummed with what could only be described as delight.

"Lincoln, Andrei," he greeted both with a nod in each direction.

So, he was on a first name basis with these two. How peculiar. I didn't peg Dracula as the type of ruler to know all of his subjects' names, so there had to be some connection there.

Estrid walked over, tossing an arm over my shoulder before squeezing me close to her. "Isn't this so exciting? Drake—oh, I'm so sorry, Dracula—is here to scout our students to potentially fill an empty spot on his board. Andrei's dad sang the praises of his son and this academy so much, he wanted to come take a look for himself."

It was like a different version of Andrei suddenly appeared, taking over the one I'd grown to know and begrudgingly care for. Pushing forward to block me almost completely, he reached out to shake Dracula's hand. "It's such an honor, your grace. My father is very kind with his praise. This academy truly is exemplary."

What prep school motherfucker stuck their foot up his ass?

Looking over at Lincoln with a 'can you believe this dude' expression, I found his face riddled with worry lines, his eyes not straying from Dracula for a single moment. He was as rigid as a metal pole, and I couldn't stop myself from gravitating towards him. Worry clenched my stomach in a tight knot.

Settling my hand on his bicep, I asked softly, "Are you okay?"

Before he could answer, Dracula pushed past Andrei to stand in front of us, spreading his arms wide. "Shall we begin? I test all potential members of the board myself, in order to determine their prowess. It'll take awhile to get through the entire class, so I figured we could start with you now, Alina."

A tingle crawled down my spine as I considered the man standing before me. This was everything I'd asked for–a single opportunity to slice his head from his body or pierce his heart. So why were my palms sweating with nerves as I nodded my head in acceptance?

"I'll stay to observe, as her professor," Lincoln nonchalantly added. "I should be here in case she has an incident similar to the one yesterday."

I tried to hide the jab to my pride that accompanied his words–he made me sound like a loose cannon who needed a babysitter. While the statement might not technically be far from the truth, I had lost control the day before, I needed this time *alone* with Dracula. Something about being in his presence was unsettling, and if I was going to even dare to take my shot, I didn't want an audience if I failed.

Thankfully I didn't need to protest.

Dracula's shoulders shook with his mirth as he rebutted, "There's no need for that. I have at least a few hundred years on her, I think I can handle it. I would also like there to be as few distractions as possible during these sessions. It wouldn't be fair to the student being evaluated if there was anyone else in the room who could sabotage their chances.

It keeps it fair for everyone. I'm sure you can agree?"

My brows shot toward my hairline at the subtle inflection in his words, suggesting that Lincoln didn't want me to succeed. My blood boiled at the implication. Why wouldn't he want me to succeed? The board position was highly sought after, and Lincoln had no idea my true motives, so I had assumed he would encourage and push me to try to reach as high as I could. He was supposed to be my mate, shouldn't that come with the territory?

I turned to gauge Andrei's expression but was met with the sight of his back as he left the room, not bothering to wish me luck or any words of encouragement. What was his deal? I understood we were being evaluated for the same position, but I'd still wish for him to do his best. Our skill would do all of the talking–there was no need for nastiness between us.

The room emptied around Dracula and I, and as I stood there staring at my self-proclaimed mortal enemy, the world fell away.

Was I really going to do this right now? I didn't feel prepared. Before I'd come to this school, I'd thought myself a skilled slayer, and I still was. But as a vampire? I knew I wasn't the strongest. Should I risk my life to take this opportunity, knowing that it may never present itself again?

Stripping off his jacket and vest, he glanced at me curiously as he switched to rolling the sleeves of his dress shirt up. “A Van Helsing, huh? I’m sure there’s an interesting story behind how you became a vampire and student at this academy.”

Was he fucking toying with me?

A snarl ripped out of my chest.

Just the sound of my family's name on his lips sparked the fire of my rage. It burned as brightly as it did the night I stood in my family's home, watching their blood coat the walls and floors crimson. My vision turned red, and for the first time, I welcomed the bloodhaze, allowing it to consume me. I needed every bit of power I could muster.

Cocking his head to the side, he lifted an elegant brow toward his perfectly styled hair. “Is there a problem?”

“I’m not here to chat,” I hissed, slicing the tip of my nail in my flesh, calling Devorare to me as I launched toward him.

This was my moment. I was going to fulfill my blood oath here and now. Devorare’s cold hilt solidified in my palm, and I basked in the sparking, red glow of her gleaming blade.

I was on him in a second, slashing Devorare viciously toward his throat. But instead of the satisfying feeling of my blade sinking into his throat, I felt myself tipping forward, falling with him as his back hit the floor with a heavy thud. Still, I persevered, digging at what felt like a shield of force around his skin. I pushed every ounce of strength I had into the motion, praying to my ancestors to not abandon me. To lend me their strength.

They didn't answer me, though, and my gut wrenched at the look of confusion marring his stupidly beautiful face. He wasn't even afraid of me, despite the fact that I held a blade to his throat. That's how fucking worthless I was.

My eyes burned, tears flowing down my cheeks and dripping onto his face as the cold reality of the situation sank in. I couldn't kill him. And he was sure to turn his ire on me, signing my death warrant just as he had my family's. All of it was for naught.

My mom.

My dad.

My grandma.

My entire family.

Skye.

"Fuck," I cried out, a strangled sob tearing from

my throat as my suppressed anguish surged through me like a tidal wave. "I'm so sorry. I failed you all."

Killing Dracula should have been straightforward. As a Van Helsing, it was what I had trained my entire life to do. Yet here I was with the edge of my sword hovering next to his throat, and no one could have prepared me for what I saw through my tear-stained vision at that moment.

I forced myself to look into his pure, black eyes, needing to show him I didn't fear him, all the way to the end. But peering into the eyes of a monster, one who had the blood of hundreds of thousands on his hands, I hated that I saw so much more than darkness in his gaze.

He stared at me with reverence and awe.

What could possibly evoke those emotions from him as he stared at me? He'd orchestrated the slaughter of my family and purposefully turned me, leaving me alone in this cold, dead world. He knew exactly what he'd done.

Desire, hot and strong slammed through me, hitting me with so much force I nearly toppled off of him. My heart pounded painfully in my chest, but I refused to give up trying to drive my sword into his throat. My gaze drifted from his throat, traveling upward until my eyes focused on his lips. His fangs were out, the tips of them pressing ever so slightly over his plush bottom lip, taunting me.

It was like I'd been hit with dark magic, something old and twisted that made me burn for the tyrant beneath me.

Our breaths mingled in the gap that divided us, and I found myself wanting to consume the very air he breathed, regardless of the blood oath I'd sworn against him.

His fingers rose to rest under my chin, applying the faintest of pressure as he tilted my head down. I tried to jerk away from his touch, to turn my gaze away from his imploring eyes, but he tightened his grip on my chin. It wasn't physically painful, in fact the touch was almost gentle, but it ate viciously at my soul.

"Why are you distraught over this revelation, Alina? It's a wondrous moment that so few ever get to experience. In all my centuries of life, I've searched relentlessly for the Queen for my board, and I've finally found you."

I didn't know what the hell he was on about, and I sure as fuck didn't care.

His black eyes stared so deeply into my soul, ripping away the barbed wire and walls I kept around it to avoid anyone seeing *me. The real me.*

Reaching up to tuck hair behind my ear, he whispered, "I began to feel again the moment my eyes settled on you. I hardly remembered what it was like to be alive before..." he trailed off as his eyes flickered above my head for the briefest of moments, seemingly lost in the memories he'd acquired through the years he'd walked this earth alone. "But when I'm with you, I feel the echo of a heartbeat within me, fluttering like you've kick-started it. You've ensnared me, Alina."

Memories of my family members' dismembered bodies, their contorted faces, and my mother's and Skye's final moments assaulted my senses, and rage swelled within me once more. I could not stop– would not stop– even if it meant my own death, my own dismemberment...my own head piked outside the home of someone who'd once loved me too.

I slipped my hand from Devorare's hilt, reaching to the waistband of my black jeans to pull out the small, silver dagger I'd taken from Lincoln's room. My eyes burned with tears I couldn't hold back. I couldn't explain the devastation touching my soul, not understanding why trying to finish the monster beneath me hurt some primal part of me.

It had to be this way. My soul would never feel

settled otherwise. Rivulets of tears poured from the corner of my eyes as a single sob came from me.

Why was I crying over this? Why did my heart ache? *He deserved this.*

With a fierce battle cry, I swung the dagger toward his throat but immediately hit the same invisible force field that seemed to rest around his body.

"Why are you trying to hurt me?" he questioned, brows knitting together as he considered me.

His tone...it was haunting. The pain of my betrayal rang through in his voice, and it sounded like it came from a place deeper than simple betrayal...it sounded like heartbreak.

I swallowed a choked, gasping sob. I gritted my teeth, putting the last of my resolve into trying to push my blade beyond the barrier protecting him. "Because I'm Alina Van Helsing, and I swore vengeance for the slaughter of my family." My chest burned with the words, throat aching with the sobs tearing from it. I heaved shaky, deep breaths, hands shaking as I asked, desperation fueling the frenzied question, "Why can't I kill you?"

"Fated mates can never kill each other, Alina," he breathed out.

And with those words, my soul died.

. . .

ORDER BOOK TWO, Bite of Betrayal, here: mybook.to/bite2

WANT to read about the other students Alina met?

Alexandra's story - Order here!

Bex's story - Order here!

OTHER BOOKS BY R.L. CAULDER

The Pack Prophecy (Completed Series)

Outcast: mybook.to/Outcast

Outlaw: mybook.to/OutlawPP

Oracle: mybook.to/OraclePP

Monarchs of Hell (Completed Series)

Co-write with M Sinclair

Insurrection: mybook.to/Monarchs1

Imbalance: mybook.to/Monarchs2

Inheritance: mybook.to/Monarchs3

Darkness Rising (Completed Series)

Desolation: mybook.to/Desolation

Detonation: mybook.to/Detonation

Devastation: mybook.to/DevastationDR

Monster's Naughty List (Standalone book)

mybook.to/Naughtylist

Inferno (Standalone book)

Co-write with M. Sinclair

mybook.to/InfernoMC

Captured by the Monsters (Standalone book)

Co-write with M.J. Marstens

mybook.to/CapturedMonsters

ABOUT R.L. CAULDER

R.L. Caulder is an International and USA Today bestselling author who lives in her writing cave away from the intense heat of the Florida sun with her husband and furry writing assistants, Meow-Meow and Winrey. Life is never boring for R.L., who has hundreds of imaginary friends constantly vying for her attention and begging for their stories to be told.

If you're looking for ways to interact with R.L., you can find her on Facebook in her group:

The Cauldron: R.L. Caulder Reader Group

www.ingramcontent.com/pod-product-compliance
Lightning Source LLC
Chambersburg PA
CBHW071417200726
48294CB00002B/424
9781962070003